KEEPING AWAY FROM THE JONESES

KEEPING AWAY FROM THE JONESES

by Bowen Craig

iUniverse, Inc.
New York   Bloomington
In association with Bilbo Books

Keeping Away From The Joneses

Copyright © 2009 by Bowen Craig

All rights reserved. No part of this book may be used or reproduced by any means, graphic, electronic, or mechanical, including photocopying, recording, taping or by any information storage retrieval system without the written permission of the publisher except in the case of brief quotations embodied in critical articles and reviews.

This is a work of fiction. All of the characters, names, incidents, organizations, and dialogue in this novel are either the products of the author's imagination or are used fictitiously.

iUniverse books may be ordered through booksellers or by contacting:

iUniverse
1663 Liberty Drive
Bloomington, IN 47403
www.iuniverse.com
1-800-Authors (1-800-288-4677)

Because of the dynamic nature of the Internet, any Web addresses or links contained in this book may have changed since publication and may no longer be valid. The views expressed in this work are solely those of the author and do not necessarily reflect the views of the publisher, and the publisher hereby disclaims any responsibility for them.

ISBN: 978-1-4401-1703-9 (pbk)
ISBN: 978-1-4401-1702-2 (ebk)

Printed in the United States of America

iUniverse rev. date: 5/12/2009

We like to think of America as a classless society...

INTRODUCTION

"He really hit a police officer?"

"No, he ran over a cop with his car. There's a difference. That was back'n Johnny B's drinking days. Had a gallon of Mr. Boston's just restin' on the passenger seat and he was sitting third in line at one of those drunk driving checkpoints out on Hull Street. So, instead of getting a DUI, he pulled over onto the shoulder and floored it… knocked the one cop up in the air and the guy landed on his head. Johnny B came racing home, sweatin' like he always does, but worse, you know. Then him and his truck hid back about a mile in the woods behind our house. Three days. I had to bring him food and bait for three days. I mean, I love my husband, but it was like havin' a pet raccoon, Miss Ethel, can you believe that?"

Ethel could believe it.

Diedre Jones had been Ethel's maid for five years, and hearing the Jones family tales of over-the-top tragedy, mind blowing disregard for Ethel's precious societal norms, and simple lack of common sense, was now just a part of her daily routine.

Diedre was standing in Ethel's living room, wielding her mop awkwardly, like an apparently uncomfortable child soldier posing for "Newsweek" with his AK-47, waiting for Ethel's measured response.

"Honestly, Dee, of course I can believe it. Compared to the time he snuck live ammo into the Civil War reenactment, that's nothing."

"Shot him five Yankees that day…of course they were from Georgia and one of them was my cousin, but he musta thought they were Yankees. Or maybe he just felt like shooting somebody. Who knows?"

Ethel knew that this question was rhetorical in nature.

CHAPTER ONE---SYMBIOSIS, SOUTHERN STYLE

It was Wednesday. Diedre Jones was cleaning the house of her favorite client/financial advisor/confidante/loan department/only rich friend, Ethel Robinson. Diedre, known to everyone simply as Dee, loved Ethel. Most of Dee's clients were just that--clients: people whose houses she and her mother cleaned while trying to mask their hatred. But Ethel was like the rich aunt who's minor royalty in your imagination.

Dee went to Ethel with her problems while she cleaned the Robinson house. Dee asked Ethel's advice about everything. Dee loved Ethel. Ethel loved Dee and loved that Dee loved her. There's also some awe, jealousy and pity mixed in there. It's classic Southern symbiosis. The rich matriarch doles out advice and bail money. The poor family cleans her house, fixes her appliances, and kisses her ass with amazing precision, usually landing those wet ones smack dab in the middle of the rich lady's lily white, heavily insured, and possibly surgically enhanced, ass. It's a lot like the "Driving Miss Daisy" set up, but nowadays the rich one isn't always white and the poor one isn't always black. Still, it works out fairly well for all parties involved....

Dee is tall, about 5'9", skinny, with shoulder-length brown hair and large, marble-sized deep-set chestnut eyes. She's a big boned woman, who is in no way 'fat', just actually big boned. Dee's quite possibly a hypochondriac, but with good reason. Ethel, once a celebrated local beauty, gave up on appearances after the birth of her second child.

She's heavy-set, around 5'3", with short cropped dyed reddish-black hair, a welcoming, matronly appearance, and an excessive, sometimes conflicting, sense of generosity and propriety.

Ethel was sitting in her adjustable chair. Ever since her adult onset diabetes flared up and her knees gave out, Ethel has relied on that wonderful contraption more and more. It's just a chair, but with a remote control which allows a seatee to be lifted into the upright position and become a standee without hurting his or her knees. It's a useful toy for the social security set. Ethel loved her chair.

This was their routine. Ethel sat, read, listened, and half-heartedly watched her favorite movies over and over again. Dee cleaned the house sporadically, pausing for smoke breaks and long talks with her modern matriarch/guru, Ethel.

"I know, Miss Ethel. I know. Sparkles ain't never really read too good. The school said that she's got a low IQ, not low enough to get her in them special classes, but pretty close. Now she's my daughter, my little girl, the only one who still remembers that I'm her mother, but still I worry about that baby."

"Oh-Oh?"

"Only baby she's got…far as I know."

"Is he out of the hospital yet?"

"Yeah. Yesterday. You just know that baby's gonna be all kinds of spoilt. He went to the hospital 'cause everybody loves him too much. Sparkles gave him some chocolate and a corndog before she went off to work. Then Johnny B and Dumpy were watching him and they gave him some of the ribs and Cole Slaw they's eating to watch the race. Then Mike got off work and was trying to feed Oh-Oh his baby food, and that's when he started turnin' blue. You know the rest."

"How many times has that baby been to the Emergency Room exactly?"

"I don't know, but all the nurses yelled his name when we came in this time."

That's usually not a good sign.

It was what Ethel didn't say that allowed her to remain friends with Dee. Some women might feel the need to tell another woman that allowing her grandchild to eat a corndog, or allowing anyone to eat a corndog for that matter, was about as healthy as feeding the baby gravel. Others might point out that if an infant has frequent flier miles at the hospital before he can eat solid food, then maybe a change in parenting style is in order. But Ethel advised only when solicited.

"Where's Hannah?"

"Downstairs."

"You mean she's downstairs working, Dee, or she's downstairs sleeping in one of my boys' beds?"

Ethel let her mind wander back to the worn copy of the well-loved, semi-literary, work of British erotica that she had been reading before the carnival arrived for one of its twice weekly visits. When Dee and her mother Hannah left the Robinson house, it was cleaner; that can't be denied. But it was also newly burdened with the current Jones problem of the week.

This week it was a recurring theme----"THE BABY". The baby, Oh-Oh, was the Jones family angel, a miracle baby, the living tablet from the top of the mountain, the gift from Jesus. His name wasn't "Oh-Oh" on the birth certificate; it was Oliver Wendell Jones. But Oh-Oh works as the prerequisite Southern nickname. The kid's already a regular at the ER, having swallowed three green plastic Army men of varying ranks, a nine volt battery, forty-seven cents in change, and the nose off one of the many pieces of taxidecor aligning the walls of the Jones family double wide. The family has yet to realize the irony of naming him Oliver Wendell.

"I'll go wake up Mom."

While Dee was downstairs, Ethel thought about the Jones family and how her life had changed because of knowing them. Ethel Robinson was a Southern princess: to the manor born, to the all girls' college shipped, to the marriage led, and to the country club driven. While by no means a snob, Ethel was snobby. While certainly compassionate, Ethel was conservative. While undoubtedly intelligent, Ethel had let her brain enter a holding pattern. Ethel's husband died after giving her ten good years of marriage, a great life insurance plan and two healthy boys. Butler, Ethel's first born, was a lawyer living in Atlanta. And Craig, her baby, was a struggling stand-up comic/waiter/motel maid/ whatever job would pay his rent and buy him enough pilsner to keep him properly tanked in between shifts at jobs where he would've felt like the biggest disappointment to a mother outside of the British royal family...if he'd cared. Craig was living in New York City, a source of constant amazement to the Joneses whenever Craig would visit home. If you've never left rural Georgia, then talking to someone who lives in New York is like talking to the small troll who lives in your pancreas.

Other than having them park her car, give her a pedicure, or beg her for money on the street and over the phone, Ethel had never really had much contact with anyone who could change a tire without calling triple A, count by NASCAR, or catch a venereal disease without leaving home. But the Joneses changed all that. At first Hannah and Dee just cleaned her house as they would any of their other customers. But Dee came to Ethel with a problem one day. Ethel fixed it. And thus a miracle worker was born in Dee's eyes. Granted, the advice was to drive her husband and his brother to the hospital and have the surgery to remove each of their right index fingers from the others' nostril instead of taking them on the road and charging unsuspecting folks two bits for a Siamese gander, but it was still good advice (Dee's husband and his brother had attempted to test the age-old friend/nose conundrum). The Joneses were fucked up, but they were fun to watch.

Hannah is Dee's mother and her boss. She's one of those 'Built Ford Tough' mountain women who shriek instead of speak, who form unshakable opinions at age sixteen, who think the devil is always right around the corner, literally, and who could probably kick your ass. From the get go, Dee's friendship with Ethel had bothered Hannah. Hannah tried to secretly despise Ethel, but Hannah, being the consummate Scotch-Irish mountain woman for whom subtlety meant waiting until your husband walked inside before hitting him with a lead pipe, couldn't keep a secret. Consequently, Hannah came over to Ethel's house to "work" twice a week, but never actually managed to do any. Everyone rebels in different ways. And since Hannah didn't clean Ethel's house, Dee was stuck having to clean the entire plantation-sized mini mansion. This was one of the things that Dee complained about. Hannah also treated Dee worse than she did her other children, another source of constant worry for Dee, and hence, for Ethel. It's like a centrifuge or one of those cheap fake horsey 'looks like it was designed by retarded carnies' toys outside of Walmart, it goes round and round.

You get the picture.

Like many Southern families, the Jones family was big. The family tree does fork, but let's just say some of the branches overlap a little. And, other than Dee's wandering eldest daughter, Charity, none of the Joneses had ever been further North than Nashville, further South than Panama City, Florida, further West than Birmingham, or further East than Atlanta.

Hannah had three children, each with a different husband. Dee's older brother, Peter, or Uncle P, is a creative junkie. Dee's younger brother, Eric, is in prison for molesting livestock, although in court he'd claimed that the goat did consent, not so much with words, but with his eyes. The judicial system has wisely decided to keep a close watch on Eric. Hannah obsessively doted on her two sons and mercilessly criticized Dee. That's just the way it is with some families.

Hannah and Dee left to call it a day, but Dee came back to Ethel's an hour later. As always, she came equipped with a brand new crisis. This time it involved Dumpy, Johnny B's brother/clone and Dee's brother-in-law. Dumpy and Johnny B are brothers in every sense of the word. They were of the same uterus, but they also think alike, talk alike, look alike, and, unfortunately for both of their wives and any bystanders, smell alike. It's hard to describe odor, but theirs is similar to hard boiled eggs dipped in bacon grease and then basted liberally with construction worker back hair sweat and just a dash of tarragon. Dumpy and Johnny B also both buy specially made pants at Sir Stout's Portly Pants Emporium. They both piously worship at the altar of NASCAR, being zealots to the point that, when local hero, Johnny Cane, retired, they both entered a two month period of mourning complete with confusion-causing matching tattoos of his head on their upper backs. They also both used to drink their homemade whiskey out of baby sippy cups, until Oh-Oh's third infant blackout made them rethink that particular policy.

After leaving work, Dee had gone home and discovered that her husband, Johnny B, was gone. Johnny hadn't worked since the heister incident at the plant a few years ago, but still managed to contribute to the family financially through his SSDI disability payments and whatever money he earned betting on the weekend cock fights at the Corner, Johnny B's regular bar/hang-out.

"I can't find him anywhere, Miss Ethel."

"Dee, calm down honey. Sit down for a sec and breathe, OK. Breathe in…breathe out."

"OK, OK, that's better, yeah."

"Did you call his parole officer?"

"A'course, Miss Ethel. He's on speed dial. I always call Officer Johan first. He's pretty nice for a foreigner."

"I thought he was from Alaska."

"That's right."

"Have you called the Corner yet?"

Dee smacked herself in the forehead in one of those exaggeratedly dramatic gestures for effect.

"Why didn't I think of that? Can I use the phone?"

Ethel grinned and nodded at Dee's unnecessary politeness. Dee had shat in Ethel's bathroom hundreds of times and had even spent a week living in Ethel's basement during Johnny B's latest jail stint, but still asked permission to use the phone or borrow a few plies of Charmin. It's a Southern thing.

After ascertaining that Johnny B was simply at his favorite local watering hole, the Corner, drinking what she thought was non-alcoholic brew, with his brother, Dumpy, Dee thanked Ethel for all of her "help" and drove off hesitantly enraged and determined to confront Johnny B in her own passive-aggressive 'life's beaten-me-down' manner. Ethel knew that she'd hear all about it next Wednesday when Dee and Hannah returned. And, as always, it'll be weird, fascinating, a little scary, and require either a bail bondsman or a preacher.

CHAPTER TWO--NOBODY KNOWS BUT JESUS

Uncle P was in the ER. While not as much of a regular as Oh-Oh, Uncle P had spent enough time in the Emergency Room that one of the beds now has his permanent ass groove and smells vaguely of chitlins and his already described sweat odor. Peter Jones, known colloquially in the family as Uncle P, was the family junkie. Every family's got one, and the Joneses were no exception. However, Uncle P was nothing if not creative, meaning that he for the most part only applied his penchant for original thought toward finding new and exciting ways to get high. Today, it was a fruit related mishap.

Uncle P had read that people scrape off parts of the peels of bananas and bake them, creating a slightly hallucinogenic smokeable intoxicant.* So, 'if you can get high off of bananas, why not coconut rinds?' was the question in Uncle P's head. There's an answer to that one, but Uncle P won't realize it until two days later when he comes out of his coma and the attending doctor explains that smoking coconut rinds **won't** get you high, but **will** land you back here in your ass groove with tubes in your arms. It wasn't exactly the deterrent that the doctor had assumed.

Dee, Ethel, Sparkles, her husband Mike, Johnny B, and the baby, Oh-Oh, took up one whole row of hospital waiting room seats. Johnny B took up two all by himself. Ethel was not exactly svelte either. And no one could accuse Sparkles of being anorexic, or even of not obeying the all you can eat regulation at Long John Silver's.

Dr. Wynn approached the assembled Joneses and Ethel.

Dee said, "It's that new doc from up North," to Ethel, whispering it as though it were an insult (which depends on your point of view).

"Hello. I'm Doctor Wynn. I've checked on Peter and the good news is that he's going to make it. He's going to be fine after a few days rest and a couple more tests."

"I thought he was in a coma?"

"He is…but it's still rest. I'm positive that he'll be up and around soon."

The family was relieved.

"Oh, that's fantastic."

"Thank you so much, doctor."

"You Jewish?"

"Um yeah, I'm Jewish, but what does that have to do wi', whatever. Anyway, the bad news is that Peter needs to stop smoking random things. Last week it was a nectarine peel. A few months ago they tell me that he was in here after injecting himself with prune juice. And, according to the chief resident, last year he checked himself in after doing something with star fruit that I'll leave to your imagination."

Dee again whispered to Ethel, "He shoved 'em up his butt."

Ethel could've done without that image.

"Well yeah, he did. Anyway, you can go home and come back in two days to pick him up. But *please* try to get him to stop smoking fruit…maybe buy him some liquor."

The family all nodded along and agreed that Dr. Wynn's plan had merit. But that might be due to the fact that Dee believed that all Jews have magical powers after misinterpreting a sermon about Moses. Since that time, she'd been writing various comedians and movie executives weekly for advice on clean living.

Ethel, Dee, Sparkles, Mike, Johnny B, and the baby were all piled in Ethel's SUV en route back to Ethel's house. Sparkles' husband, Mike, is a virtual non-talker. While not medically mute, he's one of those fifties men, one of those John Wayneish guys for whom words aren't a necessity for communication: a strong silent type. Since he lives with two very chatty women, a baby whose screams can shatter Plexiglas, and an old timey Georgia story-telling man, he couldn't get too many words in edgewise, even if he'd wanted to. Mike is skinny, wiry, tall, and has jet black hair that's always meticulously combed. He's a hard working factory employee whose life seems to be one giant hamster maze without a piece of cheese at the end. The baby was crying and his parents were both running down the list of ways to shut him up: you know, give him the breast, jangle something colorful in front of his face, sing to him, or stuff his face with whatever food-related meat by-product is nearby.

Ethel, sensing the need for someone to say something, asks a question, "So how's Oh-Oh progressing?"

Silence.

"I mean, is he trying to stand up yet, pull himself up, trying to imitate your words?"

Johnny B fielded this one, "Well, not so much with the words, but damn if he ain't a fast crawler. Dumpy and me raced him against a chicken the other day and he won. No contest."

"Daddy, you raced my baby against a chicken?"

"Gotta bet on something."

"But daddy?"

"Why you complaining? He won."

Ethel Robinson's house was located in a country clubbish subdivision called the Harringtons. A superbly designed Robert Trent Jones golf course is the centerpiece of the neighborhood. Faux antebellum/nuovo-plantation style houses that cost more than the Gross National Product of Ecuador line the course. There's a guard at the gate. There's a semi-formal restaurant. There's a nineteenth hole type bar and grill called the Wine Down for après-golf drinking binges and cocktail parties. There are people on site to wash your car, carry your bags, and give you a sponge bath if that's what you need. Ethel lives at 246 Nottingham Drive. Her house is large by normal human standards, but one of the smaller ones at the Harringtons. Still, it has three floors, two of which Ethel can't access anymore due to her knees. It's a red brick house with white trim and long, winding, purposeful kudzu vines crawling up the two outermost columns on the expansive front porch, intended to give it an anachronistic country cottage feel, which it doesn't because it's the size of four country cottages. It also has a discreet two car garage, a circular driveway, and a garden that's seen better days but still manages to produce a few delicate lilies and fierce marigolds every spring.

The inside of the Robinson household is tasteful, largely early American. The antiques are mixed with modern appliances, and foreign artifacts that say 'yes, I've traveled the world; here's the proof, and this is the best stuff I could find out there. Now, be jealous.' The basement was designed to give the kids somewhere to live that could easily be soundproofed. The lowest floor has a bathroom, a sitting room and two bedrooms left in tact for Ethel's sons when they visit. Neither of Ethel's spawn knows that a seventy year old mountain maid named Hannah sleeps in their beds when they're away. Butler, Ethel's oldest, would be outwardly horrified and secretly delighted. Craig, the youngest, would just shrug. He's had stranger stuff in his bed. All three rooms upstairs are now storage.

But the middle floor in Ethel's house, now that's the happening floor, or as happening as a level in a retired teacher and upper class professional widow's house can be in Comment, Georgia. Ethel's bedroom, bathroom, and shoe room are in the back. She has a rarely used, but still immaculately decorated, guest room, a dining room, a living room, a rec room where she spends most of her time, another bathroom, and a kitchen with an adjoining laundry room. So, that's Ethel's house.

The Jones house is easier to describe. It's a double wide trailer with five rooms: two bathrooms, two bedrooms, and one kitchen/living room/dining room/baby's room/TV room/fish gutting workshop/child whoopin' room/whittlin' facility/everything else you can think of room.

Ethel's house is, in the minds of the other Harrington residents, a lovely and slightly quaint home. In the eyes of the Joneses, it's the Empire State Building.

It's all a matter of perspective.

CHAPTER THREE--THE COURTSHIP OF SPARKLES' FATHER

It was a Wednesday. Hannah was downstairs napping while Dee was washing dishes and telling Ethel snippets of the abridged story of her love life, up to that point.

"...naw, Miss Ethel. Mom hated Johnny B, but that's prob'ly why I wanted to marry him."

Ethel smiled. "How did you two meet?"

"Oh, long story. You don't want to hear it," Dee said as she proceeded to launch into the story. "We had a class together in school, history, American history. He flirted with me, but kind of shy you know, which was weird 'cause he was a wild boy, a party boy. He played football and after the game one Friday night, we beat one of them Gordon County schools pretty bad, after the game he saw me and asked me out. At first Daddy was happy since Johnny B played ball and all, but that didn't last."

"Where'd he take you on that first date Dee?"

"Where else, Miss Ethel? The DQ. Johnny B handed me a Dilly bar and kept his hand on mine just a little too long, you know. That's when I knew he loved me. After that we went to the drag strip to watch Dumpy race. Dump used to be a legend at the strip before the wheels fell off."

"Well Dee, the wheels often do come off of our grand plans."

"No, I mean he got too fat. He sat in his drag car and the wheels fell off...but that was later. That night we watched and cheered and

Johnny B let me wear his jacket 'cause I was cold. It was nice...until he dropped me off at home. We stayed out too late and Mom was waiting for us in the driveway with a switch in her hand and her hair up in those pink teenage curlers. I can take a beating and all, but the scary thing was mom was between husbands and dating that crazy Quinton then, the Vietnam guy. And Quinton was on the roof of the trailer with his sniper rifle...again. He took a few shots at us. Thank God he was drunk or I'd prob'ly be dead. Me and mom jumped back in Johnny B's truck and we drove to the cop station and then came back with a SWAT team and got Quinton off the roof. You know Sheriff Hawkins?"

"We're in the Lions Club together."

"That's the night he lost his ear."

"Seriously?" Ethel asked with a slightly mischievous glint in her eye.

"For real. Quinton shot his ear off. He weren't the Sheriff then or they'd've probably killed poor Quint. Quinton's in the state hospital now, thank you, Jesus."

"And that was your first date? Memorable. No wonder you got married, it's almost too good of a story not to do so."

"I guess. These go in the dishwasher?" Dee asked, holding up two nice pieces of rich Southern lady requisite fancy china (the kind you keep for "company" whether they're coming in real life or only in your head).

"No, wash those by hand if you don't mind Dee. They're the good ones...so, wait, if Johnny B saved your mom's life, why does she hate him so much?"

"I wish I knew. She was grateful and all that for a while, but I think she just thought I should've married better, you know someone with money, or someone who finished high school, or well, you know."

Ethel knew.

"Mom never comes out and says nothing too bad about Johnny no more, just little mean comments, you know?"

"I know. She even tells me."

"You don't believe her, do you Miss Ethel?"

"Are you kidding, Dee? You know how much I like Johnny B. Plus, I don't like your mother any more than you do. If I could fire her and keep you, believe you me, I would."

"Who's Yume?"

"Don't worry about it. So what does Hannah say about you and your family?"

"Oh you know. She thinks she's better than us 'cause she lives up in Woodland Springs, the nice trailer park. They've got a pool, a trout pond, and all that hunting land. And we're over in Paradise Valley."

Until that very moment Ethel Robinson hadn't known that there was such a thing as a nice trailer park.

CHAPTER FOUR--THE RUN UP TO THE (WIND) FALL

The Pretty Good Market was a local jab at the national convenience store chain, The Favorite Market. And the title was fitting. It was indeed a pretty good market, not great, and almost nobody's favorite, but pretty good.

Sure there's some of the standard 'convenience' store merchandise at the Pretty Good, but there's also a lot of crap. Wait, that's redundant. There's beer, tobacco products of all varieties (including the briefly popular and best forgotten Camel suppository), and a few school supplies of the abacus/ink quill era. But there are also 'coon pelts and squirrel tails for the homemade clothing set and the 'impatient hunter who's been banned from the zoo' crew.

One of the only two employees of the Pretty Good Market, Lola Jane Copeland, had been the runner up in the 1968 Miss West Virginia pageant...and she wasn't about to let anybody forget it. In fact, all of the decorations in the PGM were pictures of Miss Lola Jane with a sash over her shoulder, a glint in her eye, and a perk in her breasts, all of which had long since faded in "real life".

Dumpy had been in love with Miss Lola Jane since the first time she sold him a log of Copenhagen for half price. Since that day, she was the primary outlet for all of Dumpy's conceivably realistic fantasies and pent up flirtation. Dumpy was technically married, only he didn't know it. Apparently, when a couple shares a residence for over seven years they're considered married. It's what's legally referred to as a

Common Law Marriage. Elaine and Dumpy had been living together for ten years. Despite having spent a sizable portion of his life dealing with the legal system, Dumpy knew surprisingly little about it. That allowed him to flirt with impunity, well, that and the fact that Elaine didn't know that Dumpy was flirting with the former 1968 Miss West Virginia runner up. She'd have been less than thrilled.

Johnny B and Dumpy were participating in one of their time-honed rituals. When they weren't at The Corner, they hung around the Pretty Good Market almost every afternoon. Since the rules for country convenience stores are, let's just say, kind of lax, Dumpy and his brother were allowed to buy individual beers, drink them outside, and then return for another. That's not technically illegal anywhere as long as there's a brown bag involved to protect the children from the knowledge that the guy living under the bridge isn't drinking Shasta after Shasta. Still, most law enforcement officials frown on selling booze to already intoxicated people. But even if the Comment Police Department had cared, there was little that they could've done. Dumpy and Johnny B are experienced drinkers. You know those guys who can drink beer after beer and never seem to show any effects at all; well that applies here. In fact, Johnny B was so good at hiding his alcohol intake that his wife thinks that he's been clean and sober for six years, despite the fact that he spends almost every afternoon in a bar. People believe what they want to believe.

The brothers' ritual included beer in individual brown bags, the full gamut of lottery tickets, gossip, and people watching, not necessarily in that order. Men gossip just as much as women, only for different reasons. Johnny B and Dumpy engage in this ritual so often that the Pretty Good Market felt that it'd be cost effective to buy them folding chairs, give them a slight discount if they reuse their paper bags, and basically cater to their every whim. Since the two of them make up close to thirty percent of the PGM's business, the store'd be crazy not to give them whatever they want. And what they want is alcohol, a slim chance to become millionaires, and heaps of good old fashioned country drama.

Seated outside the PGM, facing West for the sunset, like a 'before' shot in a Slim Fast commercial, sat two obese men.

"Hey JB, you notice anything different 'bout Lola today?"

"Uh, new haircut?"

"Naw, she wasn't wearing her dentures. Mmmm. You know how I like that."

"You know Dump. I've never said this to you before, but why come you're turned on by a woman with no teeth?"

Turning his head toward his brother disbelievingly, Dumpy said, "Come on J.B. Use your imagination. Why would a man want a girl with no teeth?"

In one of those Bugs Bunny cartoon, metaphorical light bulb turning on above the head kind of moments, Johnny B figured out the reason for one of his brother's seemingly more random sexual proclivities.

"Got it Dump. Hey, you win?"

Neither of them had won anything today. This was unusual. One of the many brilliant things about the Georgia Lottery (the best law passed in Georgia since the 'Damnit Y'all, For Real This Time, Stop Marrying Your Cousins' Act of 1924) is that the game designers did their research. Based on the formulas of other successful state lotteries, they figured out how many minor wins (win another ticket, win five dollars, win another chance to waste money you don't have) are needed in order to keep people coming back for more. It's like a No-Down-Payment on a new car deal, a get the first CD for a penny if you buy twelve more at regular price transaction, or a crack dealer giving you the first vial for free. It's capitalistic catechism and it works...most of the time. Still, the law of averages combined with the fact that the lottery coordinators don't want to have to use the wide angle lens to show winners as fat as these two guys as their poster boys, meant that today, Dumpy and Johnny B were losers. It could be argued that they were losers everyday, but definitely today.

"Naw brother, I ain't even won another dang scratcher today. You?"

"Nope. Nothing."

"Well J.B. I'm going back in. Let's give it one more try."

"Aww, you just wanna see Miss Lola Jane without her teeth."

"Well, yeah."

They each bought a few big game tickets, got a tall boy for the road, said their wistful goodbyes to the Miss West Virginia runner up of 1968, and left.

Meanwhile, at the Harringtons, Dee and Hannah were at Ethel's house for their standard Friday cleaning/bitching/passive-aggression ritual. All three Southern ladies were upstairs in the rec room. Ethel was in her beloved adjustable chair. Dee was mopping the attached kitchen area. Hannah was half-heartedly sorting the clothes for washing in the semi-detached laundry room.

Dee and her mother seemed to Ethel to be getting along better than usual today, but that was just an act. Hannah's powerful, honest, Appalachian anger is like a Jack-in –the-Box; it goes round and round inside smoothly, until all of a sudden, BAM, it's out there and it scares the shit out of the pets. Dee, on the other hand, internalizes her anger, but her breakdowns are bigger, more severe and involve kiddie pools of tears, unlike her mother's. Hannah was mad at Dee about not letting her baby-sit Oh-Oh and something about a bushel of corn. She was seething. Ethel had seen that seethe before and knew what was coming. Although this look was often on Hannah's face, Ethel couldn't read what was on Dee's. She looked gaunt and paler than usual. Ethel tried to head off what was coming at the pass.

"Hannah, the boys are coming home for Thanksgiving next week, so would you mind giving the downstairs a quick once over? It doesn't need to be perfect, but fresh sheets and towels and a little vacuuming might help."

Hannah grunted her begrudging acceptance and headed downstairs. Dee looked noticeably relieved.

"Thanks, Miss Ethel. She's about to pop."

"Oh, I know. I just don't want to be around when she does."

"Well, it's coming. She's mad about not being able to baby-sit, but she scares Oh-Oh near to death. It might be her voice, but I think it's cause her head's so big. Big heads scare babies, don't they?"

"It scares **me**."

Even banishment to the basement couldn't quell Hannah's anger. She came stomping up the stairs after two and a half minutes and positioned herself in the rec room/kitchen door frame which connects to the living and dining rooms, effectively blocking Dee's most obvious means of escape. Hannah was the Napoleon of interfamily gossip wars. She knew her strategy and was stubborn enough to stick with it to victory or to Waterloo, whichever should happen.

"I wasn't gonna say nothing, but why can't I watch the baby, Diedre? He's my great grandchild and y'all won't hardly let me see him. That ain't right and you know it!"

Hannah just stood there, expecting an answer. Dee was standing uncomfortably, shifting her weight from one foot to another.

"You wanna know why you can't see the baby, mom?"

"Yeah."

"You really wanna know?"

"I said yeah."

"It's cause you scare him. Dang ma, you scare **most** people. That voice, it's like a car skidding to a stop, or like a dying bird or something. And your head, it's huge. The baby prob'ly thinks you're a cartoon with that blimp on yer shoulders."

Hannah, momentarily speechless, stood still. Dee's face was getting redder and redder and Ethel could see a few veins beginning to show in her forehead. This was new. After one uncomfortable minute, Hannah fired back.

"It don't matter if I've got five heads. He's still family. I'm the only great grandma he's got and I should be able to see him. I won't be around forever, you know. You don't let me see him and yer gonna regret it when I'm gone."

Under her breath, Dee whispered, "Yeah, when's that gonna be, mom?"

"What?"

"Plus, he ain't my baby, momma. He's Sparkles' baby. And it's Sparkles' decision if she wants to let you see the baby or not."

The argument continued. It spiraled. It ebbed. It flowed. It paused for a smoke break. It got going again. Meanwhile, Ethel was having an ongoing internal Southern Belle debate: should I step in and stop these two poor women from fighting in my house--is it my business--it is my house--what would Scarlett do?—what would my mother do? This wasn't the first time Ethel had had this debate.

Once Dee and Hannah came back inside after a normally

tranquility-inducing, silent time-out for tobacco, they jumped right back into it. You've got to love family.

"Not letting the kid sees his MawMawMaw, that's just wrong."

"MawMawMaw? You really want the baby to call you that?"

"It don't matter what the baby calls me. He ain't barely seen me noways. Why's he need a name for me? You should just tell him I'm dead. You'd like that, wouldn't you?"

Everyone has a breaking point. And when it hit Ethel that she didn't have to let her maids fight in her own home, she stood up (without the aid of the magic Lift-o-Chair) and shouted:

"That's enough!! Hannah, go downstairs and finish the boys' rooms! Dee stay up here and wash the dishes. You two don't say another goddamn word to each other in this house today!"

Mother and daughter paused in disbelief. Neither of them had ever heard Ethel even raise her voice, much less bark orders at them while taking the Lord's name in vain. After starting to say something and then wisely stopping herself, Hannah slunk downstairs. She didn't clean anything, preferring to smoke a cigarette on the stairwell in protest and then leave by way of the downstairs back door, taking her van and Dee's ride and driving off to complain to someone who might care. And back in Ethel's rec room, Dee's face gradually turned from bright crimson to mauve to pink back to her normal pasty peach. Her breathing slowed and her heart rate went from round seven of a heavyweight bout to ten minutes after step class to student pulling all-nighter, to Calgon take me away woman in bathtub with candles and bubbles. And then she could talk and work again.

Meanwhile, at The Corner, Johnny B and Dumpy were helping PH, the owner, set up for tonight's local wrasslin' event. You know how black project kids deprived of much hope see rap and basketball as their only realistic means for getting out of the ghetto? Well rednecks see wrasslin', car racing and country music in much the same light it's their way out of the sticks. And The Corner was THE local venue for spandex-clad greatness. WWE scouts do actually come around from time to time searching for future talent.

PH had owned The Corner since 1952, when his father died in a four car pile-up on highway 73. He was ten years old and while technically not legally allowed to run a bar in the third grade, the local authorities looked the other way, and now The Corner is a salient business. PH's Christian name is Paul Harvey, but since famed radio announcer Paul Harvey is legendary around these parts, Paul thought that it'd be less confusing if he went by his initials.

PH believed in the capitalist mantra, 'The Customer is Always Right...unless he's a Yankee', and decorated his bar accordingly. Luckily, PH's tastes tended to be in congruence with his customers. In other words, he's just as red as the guys he serves. As such, The Corner is decorated with pictures of PH in his local wrestling star heyday, various country music legends of the George Jones/Dolly Parton era, the country-bar requisite Robert E. Lee portrait, and a smattering of WWE 'actors' posters. Those pro wrestlers really don't get the respect they deserve for what they do. I mean it's about as American an activity as you can get. There's showmanship, fake violence, skin-tight clothes, steroids, girls in bikinis, and a lot of shit-talking. If that ain't America, then what is?

Dumpy, Johnny B, and PH were drinking homemade wine as they slowly turned a country bar into a country stage with a bar. It's not that difficult, but does involve an invention whose time has largely passed except in a few remote bars: chicken wire. Five years ago Ken "The Cougar" Wendall, was hit by a flying tall-boy can while engrossed in a cageless match with Joey "The Jaguar" Thompson. Since then they've all been cage matches.

"Hey PH, who's up for tonight?"

Setting down the silver colored, metal folding chair he was carrying in order to think, PH thought. Eventually, "Oh yeah, uh, there's a warm up with Killer Billy from down the street and that Mexican kid, Suarez. And the main event's Gerald versus Robby."

"Again?"

"They're brothers. People eat that crap up."

"Yeah, but they've faced each other what, ten times?"

"At least."

"So how 'bout some new blood?"

"I tried, boys. I was all set to have our first girl on girl tonight, and you know they'd be stumbling out of the woods for that one, but then one of them backed out. Still Nancy Lynn said she's go up 'gainst a guy if he's small. I'd ask one of you two, but…"

"Don't spare our feelings, PH. You can call us fat."

"Not me."

"No Dump, you're fat. It's time to face it."

"Elaine says I'm just big boned."

"It ain't yer bones that's fat, Dump. It's your fat."

"Aww, you're fatter than I am, J."

And that debate raged until PH made them both take their shirts off and, after close inspection of their respective man breasts, decided that it was too close to call. While some skeptics might call this pointless, or at least truly disgusting, it was the birthplace of PH's best marketing scheme since "Bring Your Dog to the Bar Tuesdays." The Corner's weekly, "Just How Fat Are You?" contests, enjoyed brief popularity until the weight-gaining reality show, "How Much Lard Would You Drink for Ten Thousand Dollars?" stole their thunder.

While PH was testing the mat strength, ensuring that the ropes were taut and checking his beer supply, Dumpy and his brother took an undeserved break.

"J, you see the way Lola Jane looked at me when we was leaving?"

"Dump, give it up, man. She always flirts with you. You pay her salary. That don't mean…"

"You don't know that, and come on, you're my brother, don't kill my dreams man…hey, you win anything in the lotto on our last round?"

"Naw, but I bought a few of the big game tickets."

"What's that up to now?"

"Ten million and change."

"Damn."

"Yeah, damn."

In Woodland Springs, the 'nice' trailer park in Comment, GA, Hannah and her new husband, Nestor, were just coming home from their respective days at work. Nestor works on a construction crew, usually on the roof. His amazing sense of high altitude balance is legendary, at least among the Spanish speaking members of his crew, namely he and his cousin, Paco. Nestor was Hannah's fifth husband. She's been through almost the entire litany of betrothed archetypes. She married her high school sweetheart, Brian James Redmond, and they had Uncle P. But Brian left Hannah to follow his dream with the Cirque de Southern Alabama. Her second husband was a rebound, a safe guy who wouldn't ever leave her, but that was mainly because he had no legs. She left him after pushing him around for a month. He did give her Diedre though, and was an interesting sexual partner. Hannah's third husband, Big T, or Tyrone Biggins, stayed with her for five years, although Hannah was unaware that Big T, an East coast trucker, had seven other families scattered up and down the Eastern seaboard. He gave her Eric, Dee's younger brother and current Comment prison inmate.

After Hannah discovered Big T's other families, she left him and stayed single for almost three years, a personal best. That was until she met Clayton F. Reed, a traveling salt water taffy salesman and first class lothario. They were married and divorced within a month. Disconsolate over her lack of luck in love, Hannah met Nestor one day at the Piggly Wiggly. He was happy to provide a shoulder she could cry on. She was happy to provide legal status. He was elated to have a place to live where he could hunt, fish and keep chickens in the yard. She was contented to have a man in the house who wouldn't leave her (a fact she discovered after adding the INS to her speed-dial). It was a pretty good marriage. Neither of them could speak the other's language, but love isn't about words, not really. In Nestor and Hannah's case, love is about having someone at home to pretend to listen to your bitch session.

"...he's my dern great grandkid. Nestor, you hear me?"

"Oh yes."

Hannah was cleaning chicken breasts and gizzards for tonight's feast while Nestor was rapidly getting undressed in hopes that Hannah would perform her wifely duties.

"I mean, I gave her a job, a career, heck I gave her life for God's sake."

"Oh yes."

"She's my daughter. I could've let her no leg daddy raise her, but no I thought she'd want someone who's responsible, someone who can get a job other than second base, but no, she just, Nestor what are you d', I'm cooking, honey, can't you wait, oh what the heck..."

I'd go into details, dear readers, but trust me, you don't want to know.

Enjoying the time honored ritual of a shared post sex cigarette, Nestor and Hannah lay on their queen sized bed and talked. Unbeknownst to Hannah, Nestor was unfavorably comparing Hannah's sexual prowess to that of his other wife, who was busy raising his kids in Chiapas. Of course, Hannah didn't know this since she hadn't bothered to learn any Spanish other than the commands for "Get out of my house", "Give me your paycheck", and "No sex today". Meanwhile, Hannah was continuing to vent about her situation with Diedre and the baby. As they were both putting their clothes back on and Hannah was restarting dinner, her son, Uncle P, knocked on the trailer door.

"Hey honey," Hannah said as they hugged hello. While initially against the idea of his mother marrying a Mexican, Uncle P had quickly come to respect Nestor. They had shared interests. Both of them enjoyed hunting, fishing and catching a buzz. Nestor preferred the smooth shoulder-slumping relaxation that is America's national drug, alcohol, whereas Uncle P liked to experiment, but they both ended up in the same place, often in the same dumpster. Also, for the most part, neither of them listened to what other people were saying. They were a good match.

"Nestorino, what up?"

"Oh yes."

Hannah fed her son cookies, chocolate chip, as she had since he was little. We all regress at least a little when we see our mothers.

"Ma, tell Dee thanks for visiting me in the ER. I don't remember it or anything, but it's nice having a sister who cares."

"Half-sister."

"Whatever."

"I'm fighting with her again."

"Dang it, ma. Come on. Why don't y'all just stop working together? You might actually get along."

"We'll see. Have you talked to Eric lately?"

"Hmm. Oh yeah. **That's** why I was here. I saw Eric yesterday at the jail. He asked if his mommy would send him a care package."

"Like candy and stuff?"

"Yeah. He asked for cigarettes, cookies, shampoo and any gerbils you can spare."

"Ha, ha, ha…that boy. Hey can you stop by and pick it up say day after tomorrow?"

"Yeah, sure ma. So what's the new deal with you and Dee?"

"Oh nothing really, just Sparkles don't want me seeing the baby."

"That ain't right."

"Don't I know it?"

"Hey, ma. I know this isn't yer strong point and all, but can you try and be sweet to Sparkles? You're mean as a snake to that girl."

"Well she's stupid."

"I know that. Shoot, dogs know that, but ain't like she can help it. She's yer granddaughter. And since nobody's seen Charity for what, three years now, she's the only granddaughter you've got around."

"I'm still hoping you and Shirley will give me a present one of these days."

"Can't do it ma. Remember the court ordered vasectomy they gave me a few years back?"

"Yeah, but you can untie your tubes."

"How, ma? How'm I gonna do that? The law says I can't have kids. A doctor ain't gonna go breaking the law. So what, am I supposed to do, home surgery?...wait, I wonder if they'd give me pain pills for home surgery. Maybe…it's possible…you know, mom, this idea's pretty good…I could do it, untie my own tubes…sure…."

And Uncle P continued to look at the rarely viewed bright side of do-it-yourself-home-reproductive-surgery as he made his way out to Nestor's work shed to sniff paint. Peter had his biggest revelations while huffing paint--that's when he figured out that aliens don't own a time share in his colon, when he discovered that he didn't in fact have the ability to fly, and when he discovered that passing out in front of city hall with your head in a bucket of eggshell white will land you in jail.

Hannah, who's been in denial about her eldest son's raging drug problem for forty years, hummed a song about Jesus while she lovingly prepared a care package for her youngest son, about whom she's also in denial.

CHAPTER FIVE---WE GATHER TOGETHER TO ASK THE LORD'S BLESSING

Thanksgiving, what a strange holiday! We get together with relatives we haven't seen since last year, eat a shitload of food, gloss over historical genocide, get a little drunk, fight with our families, and pass out watching football. God bless America!

You could feel the anticipatory energy in the Robinson house. Ethel loves her children. Butler, her oldest, a lawyer living in Atlanta, comes home to Comment intermittently to comfort his mother, use her washer and dryer and eat free food. But Craig, who's been living in New York City, hadn't been home for a year and a half. So, Ethel truly had something for which to be thankful. She was also thankful for her adjustable chair for its unwavering support, her Volvo for the rich liberal street cred it provided, and the fact that she was going to be Jones-free for an entire weekend. She loved them in her way, but sometimes you just need time away from back to back to back tragedy and poverty.

The Robinsons eat Thanksgiving dinner at what used to be called 'supper time'. It's strange how we've changed the definition of dinner and all but dropped supper from the rotation, but the one constant in life, and I think the cast of "Different Strokes" will back me up on this one, is that things change. Anyway, the Robinson's eat at around four. And the Joneses, in their ongoing attempt to become the Robinsons, now also eat at four. They say imitation is the sincerest form of flattery, but then again they also say an apple a day keeps the doctor away, and even if you throw it just right, those white-coated, stethoscope wearing, God-complexion having bastards keep coming.

At three P.M. that afternoon, both of Ethel's children had made it home. Butler came alone. Craig brought his new NYC girlfriend, Sara. Sara is five foot three, wiry, energetic, New York to the core, witty, dyed-blonde, a little crazy but in a good way, and pretty in a slightly haggard, Hollywood starlet on the third day of a week long coke bender kind of way. Being a native New Yorker, Sara's much more direct than the entire population of the Harringtons put together. Craig had attempted to coach her on Southern etiquette on the plane ride down, but it just all seemed so wrong to her. Sara's family talks about their various ailments and impending death at all family gatherings. It's just a part of the meal, like potatoes.

After an initial mother hug and putting their respective luggage away, Craig and Butler began setting the table. Sara was finishing up any last minute food preparation. Ethel sat in her chair and made small talk with Sara as she conducted this little annual culinary symphony.

"Sara, you're originally from New York City, is that right?"

"Uh-huh. Why, are you going to lynch me?"

Ethel laughed. She was old enough to have seen the last actual lynching in Comment. It was 1939. Ethel's grandfather was a Klansman who thought that every adolescent girl ought to see a lynching as a natural part of her education. Thankfully, that attitude is on the wane, not gone by a long shot, but going.

"I'm just curious, honey."

"Well, I was born upstate, but my parents moved to Brooklyn when I was two, so I don't remember it. I'm a city girl."

Meanwhile Craig and Butler fell immediately back into their pattern. It's what brothers do. And in the case of the Robinson boys, what they do is sarcasm and subtle jabs. They were setting the only used once a year 'dinner' table and catching up in their own way.

"So, Butler, still in Atlanta, huh? You know I couldn't help notice that you didn't bring a date and that you live in the fastest growing gay city in the world. Interesting…"

"Ya know Craiggers, that would've been funny a few years ago. Hell it <u>was</u> funny a few years ago, but since I turned thirty, everyone really does think I'm gay. It's messed up, but if you're over thirty and single then everyone in Comment thinks you're a butt pirate."

"Butt pirate. Ha." You have to laugh at the image of a rectal swashbuckler. Or, well, you don't, but these two do. And then Craig launched into a spot on imitation of a gay pirate claiming the high school wrestling team as his lawful booty.

"What about you, little brother? What's the deal with this girl? Wait, she's not the stripper you were telling me about, is she?"

"Huh? Oh no and shhhh. No strippers are named Sara. Wait, that's not true. But no, she's a grad student...behavioral psychology."

"Cool?"

"Of course she's cool. I'm getting out of the only attracted to girls who are insane phase, I hope."

"So Sara's not crazy?"

"Oh no, she's crazy, just not homicidal. It's improvement. I take it you remember Tasha."

"Hard to forget a girl who taunts your pets until they commit suicide."

"Poor Fluffy, he was so happy before he met her. Look Butler, I know Tasha was wacked-out and all, but you still could've been nicer to her."

"I love you, little brother; you know I'd do anything for you, but I'm only a man."

"Really, you call yourself that despite the cross dressing?"

Faking laughter, "Oh, it hurts. You're just so damn funny. Is this what you do on stage in comedy clubs?"

"No, I mime scenes from the Civil War."

"OK, <u>that</u> was funny."

Meanwhile, at the Paradise Valley trailer park, the Joneses were also preparing to give thanks in the traditional manner, by overeating and yelling at your relatives. In order to save on meat costs, Dumpy and Johnny B had ventured out to find a good deal on meat. Not finding the Piggly Wiggly prices low enough, they decided to be more like the Pilgrims and kill their own meat. Well, first Dumpy suggested killing a Piggly Wiggly employee for his meat, but Johnny B knew that while killing bag boys isn't completely frowned upon, it's still not legal. The kid was pretty stringy anyway.

Firmly ensconced in their deer stand/really cool fort, the two portly brothers waited for a buck large enough to feed their ever-growing extended family. They'd placed the deer stand pretty much in the middle of the trailer park, not the best place for deer, but it did make them look cool.

"I bet if we had killed the grocery kid, we could've passed him off as venison."

"You really want to feed your family a person. That ain't right, Dump."

"I'm just sayin' it'd be quick. I ain't seen no deer all day."

"I know. Wait, wait. It's not exactly a four pointer, but look, there's three turkeys."

"You sure they're turkeys? They could be kids in their Thanksgiving costumes."

"Kids don't dress up for this holiday, Dump. They're turkeys; they're food."

"Hold up Johnny. Those're probably the Gonzalezs' chickens, the ones they keep in their yard."

"Well shit, Dump. They been here five damn years. They ought to know better'n to let their chickens run loose in November. Everybody in The Valley's got a gun."

"So it's like Manuel gave us permission to kill his turkeys."

"Now you got it."

Twelve shots, three cigarettes, and five goddamns later, they had indeed killed three treasured Gonzalez family pets. And they felt like men.

As dying traditional gender roles dictate, men kill animals outside while women cook the fixins inside. And the Joneses had an underlying sense of traditional values. Granted, the wife worked while the husband didn't, but that never seemed to bother Johnny B.

Inside, Dee, Sparkles, and Dumpy's common law 'wife', Elaine, prepared Jones family traditional dishes. Elaine was a histrionic woman, prone to exaggeration, outlandish displays of emotion, and not above fist fighting with Dumpy in the middle of church or throwing auto parts at his head at the slightest provocation at K-Mart.

Elaine and Dee prepared some of the Jones family's traditional Thanksgiving dishes: Stuffing Surprise, Ding-Dong bundles, yams in hollowed out orange peels topped with mini marshmallows, Dee's famous Twinkie Casserole, Pixie Stick Soufflé, and, of course, Kool-Aid (just like the Indians did). Dee's Twinkie Casserole has been a hit since it was first, accidentally, discovered. Much like penicillin, Shrinkie-Dinks, and anal love beads, the popularity of Dee's Twinkie Casserole was the result of a fortunate accident. Sparkles left a Twinkie in the oven and Dee turned it on to warm it up for dinner. When Dee opened the oven door she discovered a cooked Twinkie in the shape of a cow. Since then, she's been cooking and molding Twinkies into various animal shapes once a year on the last Thursday of November and then calling it a casserole. If only Hostess had known, they would've made her a spokesperson or perhaps had her killed.

Sparkles kept an eye on the baby as she and her husband, Mike, set the table with take-out plastic ware and Ethel's old glasses. Sparkles had given Oh-Oh his new toy, a Ritalin laced sugar lick, and let his brain sort it out. Oh-Oh loved his new toy. Dee was still thinking about her fight with Hannah; it had moved to the back of her mind, but it was still there.

"Sparkles, you just don't know how lucky you are to have me as a momma."

"I know, ma."

"No you don't. How could you? You've always had a good momma so you got nothing to compare it to."

"I guess you're right. Mike, sweetie, the baby's eyes are glazing over again, take away his sugar lick. Oh hey, mom, Uncle P said that Charity's coming tonight. Is she?"

"Dunno. That's what I heard, but you know your sister. She might show up with a pack a wild dogs; she might show up drunk as Cooter Brown; she might not show."

"Yep. That's Charity."

Back at the Robinson house, a respectful, barely religious prayer was being uttered for a respectful, barely religious family. Like many other families in the Eastern United States who want to head fake in the direction of religion, but not actually dedicate their lives to it, the Robinsons are Episcopalian. [[Episcopalianism: Catholicism without the religion.]] You still get to drink real wine in church (and lots more at home); you get some of the pomp, circumstance and incense; you get a twenty minute homily instead of having to take No-Doze to stay awake through an hour-and-a-half moral harangue; and then you get more wine. There's some talk of Jesus, but it's not all Jesus, all the time like most other Christian sects.

"Dear Lord, please bless this food and us to thy service. Please take care of Craig in sin city and forgive him his many, many sins including the one with the Silly String and those poor goats, and, please Lord, watch over our mother, Ethel, and keep her healthy and happy. Also, please keep the Joneses away from the house this year. All of this we ask in your son, Jesus', name. Amen."

"AMEN."

"Nice one, Butler. I think God appreciates it when you make a bestiality joke in the middle of a prayer."

"What? The goat comment. Trust me, little brother, God's got a sense of humor. I mean look at yourself in the mirror naked sometime."

Although she's a pretty cool woman with a good sense of humor, it wasn't immediately obvious to Sara that pretty much everything that Craig and Butler said to each other is sarcastic. She leaned over to ask Ethel:

"They're joking, right?"

"I hope so, honey. I gave up on religious training for those two pretty early. I think God doesn't want them in His houses of worship."

"Wait, mom, does that mean that you think we're both going to hell?"

"Noooo…well, maybe. I just failed in that aspect of motherhood… that's what I really think."

"Well that's good, momma, cause it's not like I go to church in New York."

"You might want to think about it, Craig. They've got some beautiful old churches up there. You could take Sara."

"Mom, Sara's Jewish."

"Well, then maybe she could take you to Temple. Are you religious, dear?"

"I got bat mitzvahed, but no, not really."
"What about your parents? Have they met Craig yet?"
"They have."
"And they liked him?"
"Well..."

Craig had an inkling about what Ethel was hinting at, but, politely, not saying. Sara knew the deal. As has been the habit of so many mothers, Ethel Robinson wanted her kids to settle down, and while she didn't actively try and arrange a marriage old-school India style, she did want her sons to family up and start pumping out the grandkids. Since he realized that nearly universal mother fact, Butler hadn't brought a date home, not wanting to disappoint his mother nor strengthen any pre-existing marital ideas in the heads of his dates. But Craig was better able than his brother to let things just roll off his back. Sara knew that her parents would probably forbid her to marry a gentile, and she did care, but she wasn't thinking about marriage yet in any sense other than the abstract. Sara assumed she'd marry a nice, stable Jew one day, but that was still pretty far down the imaginary road in her head, and she wasn't especially looking forward to it. She and Craig meshed well, throwing each other loving looks across the cheese-laced, chunky mashed potatoes and touching each other's legs discretely under the mahogany table, not as foreplay per se, just play.

Ethel's mother, Mrs. T., was also in attendance. She lives down the road in the one posh "retirement village", which conveniently overlooks the two cheap and ugly death prep homes. Things don't change. Even the octogenarian rich look down on the equally aged poor. Mrs. T. was once the stern task-mistress who ruled the family with an iron tongue (it's just an expression, her tongue's not made of iron; it's mostly copper). But since Mrs. T. turned ninety-five, she's mellowed considerably. Nowadays, she doesn't talk much but still manages to make her occasional wishes known. Mrs. T.'s still judgmental and holds on loosely to a dying Southern sense of propriety and moral values, but, as I say, she mellowed after her third stroke.

Every family has its holiday traditions. Due to the fact that Ethel Robinson was an English professor by trade and hence harbored a barely concealed secret desire to be a North-Eastern intellectual, the

Robinson's play the always dreaded 'Name That Quotation' game. That's the Robinson tradition.

"Y'all know what time it is?"

"Of course, momma."

THE CODE--E=Ethel, S=Sara, B=Butler, Cr=Craig. Mrs. T needs no code since she's mute.

E--"If this is the best of all possible worlds, what are the others like?"

B--Oooh, tough one. I'm going to go with Oscar Wilde.

E--No

Cr--Got to be a beat poet. Ginsburg?

E--No. Come on. This one's not that hard. Sara?

S--Voltaire. It's from Candide.

E--Very good, dear. One point to Sara.

B--What are we playing to?

E--We're playing until you stop ending sentences with prepositions.

B--For real, mom.

E--First to five. Winner doesn't have to clean. OK, next. "What nobler employment, or more valuable to the state, than that of (one) who instructs the rising generation?"

Cr--Sounds like you, mom.

B--No, Cicero.

E--One for Butler. Next, oh, let's see. "Give me the splendid silent sun with all his beams full-dazzling."

B--Thoreau?

Cr--Walt freaking Whitman.

E--And we're all tied at one a piece. I know this one's been paraphrased quite a bit, but "Those who are ignorant of history are doomed to repeat it"

S--Ben Franklin?

E--No dear.

B--George Santayana.

E--That's two for Butler. Although there is some controversy about...

Meanwhile, in Paradise Valley, the Jones family was just beginning its meal with a more traditional Southern prayer.

"Lord, we just wanted to say thank you for all the good stuff you've given the Joneses. Thank you for this delicious meal. Thank you for providing Adam and Eve with Ding Dong seeds in your garden so that they could go into my wife's famous Ding Dong Bundles. Thank you for our good health. Thank you for letting us be born Southern by your grace. Thank you for my deer stand. Thank you for Miss Ethel. Thank you for them jacked-up truck tires. Thank you for Oh-Oh. Thank you for yams. Thank you for letting us at least get through the meal before The Rapture comes, and when it does, please let us all come to heaven so we can see grandpa Jim again, and Dale Earnhardt, and Hank Williams, the original Hank, and John Wayne, but please let us finish the Twinkie Casserole first…oh and thank you for keeping Hannah out of the house tonight. AMEN."

"AMEN."

"Johnny, darn it all to heck, why do you have to insult my mother in the middle of the prayer? You really think God likes that?"

"I think God hates her too."

"If he's got ears, he does."

"That ain't right, Dumpy."

"Oh come on Elaine. You've said worse about her."

"Yeah, but not in front of the Lord. Sorry Dee."

"I'm used to it."

Just as the stuffing, bacon wrapped green beans and very, very fresh turkeys were making the rounds among the family, the wayward eldest Jones daughter, the prodigal chick, Charity, walked in with a groan, dragging a large, green Army style canvas bag behind her.

"Hey, y'all!"

"Oh my God."

"Charity!"

"It's a Christmas miracle."

"It's not Christmas."

"OK then it's just a miracle."

After a rousing group hug, the sheer weight of which would have broken most non-industrial scales, the family settled back down and began catching up. Charity Angel Jones is a homely looking girl whose appearance belies her inner sense of curiosity and rebellion. She's a tomboy, but naturally feminine enough that boys and girls alike enjoy being around her. Far and away the most common adjective used to describe Miss Charity is curious, although sometimes they mean 'curious' in the way that the Green Party of Georgia is curious, or the way that the one openly lesbian couple in a small town is curious. Charity is 5'1", stocky, with thick, muscular legs, shoulder length mahogany hair rounded out with wispy bangs, and large, searching auburn eyes. She has less of a sense of personal space than anyone in Comment other than the one guy who rubs up against people's genitals at the bus stop. Charity's a whirlwind, so when she casually strolled into her family's home after a three-year absence, commotion ensued.

As I was saying, once the group hug reached its preordained twenty second time limit (after that hugs start to get a little creepy), they all sat back down, pulled up a chair for her and set her a place at the table complete with a rhinoceros shaped Twinkie.

"Charity, tell us about your adventures."

"Yeah girl, where all you been in three years?"

"Let's see, Alabama, Louisiana, Texas, Arizona, Arizona's fun. Got as far as San Francisco before I remembered that I hadn't been home in, what'd you say Sparks, three years? My God y'all, has it been that long?"

Dee physically had to restrain herself from leaping over the table and smothering her eldest with an uncomfortably long mommy hug. Johnny B was all smiles. And the baby now had yet another candy supplier.

"Enough about me. I'll spill it all in the next few days. What's the Comment gossip?"

Elaine, being privy to more gossip than the rest of them due to her job as a local 911 operator, launched into it. She hadn't really understood the non-disclosure agreement anyway.

"Oh my Lordy, there was Cousin Juniper in Marietta; he got mauled by a German shepherd."

"No Elaine, the guy was black and I think he was a truck driver."

"I meant the dog, Dumpy. There was no guy. And Charity, you remember Mr. Bradbury down the road? He got a divorce from Ilene, so she moved in with Irwin next door and so Irwin's wife moved in with Mr. Bradbury, it was like that reality show with the wife swapping. You wouldn't swap me, would you, Dumpy?"

"You're not my wife."

"And let's see, Charity, the mayor, the old one not the new lady mayor, or mayorette or whatever we supposed to call her, the old mayor didn't run again because he took money from some construction company and let them build the new courthouse. I didn't really understand the whole thing. Oh, and Dee over there had it out with Hannah the other day at Ethel's house, and then there's…"

"For real, mom? You and mawmaw got into a fight? Like a really real fight? Pulling hair? Nails? Or just words?"

"Well, words. I don't want her coming around the baby, and we got into it at Ethel's. Ethel got maaadddd. I've never seen her mad, but the good news is I think she's gonna fire mom and just keep me on. Oh my God, sweetie, it's just so good to see you."

"Now we've all got something to be thankful for."

"Did you really just say that, Dump? Or was it Charlie Brown? It sounded like Charlie Brown."

Dumpy was polite and loved his family to the point that, although he was currently hungry enough to devour a slow-moving live zebra, he was willing to pause long enough to wish his niece welcome, but his prominent stomach was beginning to rumble again.

"Charity, great to see you, love you and all that, but let's eat."

"Amen!"

While the Robinson's were cleaning the dishes and storing them away for future use, the Joneses were participating in some of their family rituals. Like the Robinsons, the Joneses had their own holiday trivia game tradition. Theirs involved matching NASCAR drivers to their sponsors, but it's still a memory test. They also had a money saving Secret Santa pick a kindred name out of a black Intimidator hat ritual and a post meal prayer ritual, thanking the Lord for whatever they'd forgotten to mention pre-meal.

"Did you meet any famous people in California, Charity?"

"Uh no, wait, kind of, I met some Chinese looking spiritual guy, and he's good and that lady on the radio, Dr. something, Jewish lady, the one who's always telling girls they're sluts and going to hell. I hate her."

"Wait a minute young lady. We don't badmouth Jews in this house."

"Sorry, mom. I forgot the rules."

CHAPTER SIX---AND THE WINNER IS.....

Johnny B and Dumpy were sitting in matching lime green folding lawn chairs in the parking lot of the Pretty Good Market, drinking PBR tallboys, talking about Charity, Thanksgiving, the lovely Miss Lola Jane Copeland, the possibilities for leftover holiday food combinations, the weather, and the lottery. Dumpy won on nine consecutive scratch-off tickets, a personal record. Johnny B had bought five straight losers before giving up and just buying a few big game tickets. He would have to win vicariously through his brother, who was convinced that Miss Lola Jane would go out with him if he were to win ten in a row. But Dumpy's luck ended at nine. He still asked her out, and she again politely said no, which only fed into his steadfast belief that ten winners in a row equals sex with his fantasy woman.

Meanwhile, at the Harringtons, Diedre Jones was sitting in Ethel's living room, talking. Sparkles and Oh-Oh were also there. The baby was tormenting Ethel's cat, Grendel.

"Naw, it was a good holiday. I told you Charity's home. She's gonna stay for a few weeks. I'll bring her by. Sparkles, get the baby to stop messin' with that cat. Cat's gonna get mad and scratch him after 'while. I got cat scratch fever once when I was little."

"I believe they immunize for that now, Dee."

"Still girl, pick up that baby and get him away from that cat. Wait, Ethel, can't babies get sick from eating cat doo-doo?"

"Probably, but does Oh-Oh normally eat animal droppings?"

"Well maybe. The kid ate two old wigs, so ya never know."

Although she wasn't expected, Hannah came storming in through the front door. Like a lion trapping a gazelle in a grove of bushes in the ritzy upper-middle class section of the Savannah, Hannah stationed herself in the doorway from the kitchen/den to the living room, blocking any escape.

"If it ain't my ungrateful daughter."

"Uh, hey, mom."

"Don't you 'hey mom' me, young lady. This is the first time in what, fifteen years that y'all didn't invite me for Thanksgiving. That hurts, Dee."

"I'm sorry momma. I am, but it's not all up to me."

"Yes it is."

The process of anger building in Ethel Robinson is an interesting and highly regimented process. First she starts thinking what should I do in this situation, then what's the proper thing to do, then what's the Christian thing to do, then what's the compassionate thing to do, then her face gets red and she screams in exasperation. It's rare, but it's always the same. She was still in the 'what's the proper thing to do' phase.

"Momma, listen. If you calm down, wait a week and come over and apologize to Johnny B and maybe to Elaine too, then I'm sure they'll forgive you and you can come to Christmas. You could go visit Sparkles in jail too. She got pulled for some old warrants the day after Thanksgiving. Just say you're sorry and…"

"For what? I should say I'm sorry for something I didn't do wrong?"

"If you want to come to Christmas, yeah."

Ethel was now in the 'what's the compassionate thing to do' phase.

"Maybe I don't want to come to Christmas. Nestor and me had our own little Thanksgiving and Peter came. So there."

"Great, mom. I'm happy for you, but don't Mexico have different holidays?"

"Sure I guess, but I was cooking, so we celebrate America stuff. I could've cooked for you too. You know my beans are better than yours."

And now Ethel's face was changing from a February outdoors in Boston pink to a baby picture book 'fire engines are this color' red. It should only be another few seconds...

"The heck they are, mother. People eat my beans 'cause they like 'em, not just 'cause they're scared of you and your dang big head hollering!"

"Why you little…"

That was it. Using her trusty orthopedic cane to raise and then steady herself, Ethel turned toward Hannah.

"OK, that's it! I'm sick of this crap. Hannah, you're fired. I'm sorry, but you are just a horrible, horrible maid and not a good person and well, basically, I don't like you."

"Ya, you're firing us, Mrs. Robinson?"

"No. I'm firing you. Dee can stay."

"But, uh, well, OK, fine. I don't want to come by your snobby little richie rich neighborhood anyway. And you," Hannah said, pointing a shaking, calloused finger at her daughter, "you're not my daughter anymore. Stay away from me and all our clients."

And with those dramatic final words, Hannah stormed out of the house, slamming the door behind her (twice for effect). Her tires squealing, she drove out of the Harringtons like Jr. taking a curve at Talladega. Sparkles was speechless. Oh-oh was terrified. Dee looked momentarily relieved, but that quickly turned to worry. And Ethel had to sit down and catch her breath.

"Diedre, honey, could you pour me a small glass of wine? I need it. Pour yourself one too, dear."

"Y, yeah, yeah, of course."

After a five minute silence where Ethel sipped her wine, Sparkles tried in vain to comfort a baby who was too scared to cry and Dee paced the house nervously, thinking of the implications of the fight, they began to speak again.

"Mrs. Robinson, thank you for keeping me on, but now you're my only client. Ya know that, right?"

"I do now. But that's OK, honey. I can get some of my neighbors to hire you. They're always complaining about their help and they'd love you. They wouldn't have if you came along with Hannah, but trust me, they will now. Don't worry about that aspect of this. I can't do anything to help you with your family situation, but as long as I'm breathing, you've got a job."

Diedre Jones is, at heart, an emotional person. Since Dee is basically the glue which holds her family together, she often has to sand down her emotions in order to keep the peace in her family, but deep down, she's a gusher. And, after an adrenaline rush the likes of which Dee hadn't felt since they opened Dollywood, she was in no place to control her emotional outbursts. Hugging Ethel with all of her considerable strength, Dee began sobbing on her shoulder. This, in turn, made Ethel cry, which made Sparkles cry. Oh-Oh shrugged and went back to torturing the cat.

Back in Paradise Valley, Johnny B., Dumpy, and Mike were playing an out-of-date, but nonetheless special, board game called Commentopoly. For a brief period in, I believe, the 1980s, Parker Brothers, Milton Bradley or whoever makes the game Monopoly had a brilliant marketing brainstorm. They decided to individualize the game, applying the same rules and principles to towns other than Atlantic City. Maybe it was somebody else's idea. I don't know. But I know that if you lived in Baltimore, then you could, and presumably still can, buy Baltopoly, or in Orlando, Diznopoly, or in Comment, Georgia, Commentopoly. That's the game that Dumpy and Johnny B were playing this afternoon while the wind was whipping through their trailer park and the television was making vague background noises.

"I got Big Bob's Feed Store. I'm buying it, hoss."

That's the equivalent of North Carolina Avenue on the original-- one of the coveted dark greens.

"Aiight. That's an eleven for me and I'm landing on Davis' Hunting Supply and Christian Book Store. Buying it."

That's the equivalent of Baltic Avenue--in the low rent district.

"I'm up and I landed on your Freda's Fixins. I'm out of cash, but the rules says that I can barter with these two goats."

"OK, I'll take your goats, but next time your better have something better to trade…a rifle, or some womens."

Behind the heated game, local TV anchorwoman, LaFarrah Jefferson, was pulling bingo numbers out of an oversized hopper as a warm up to the big game announcement.

"I'm up. Rolled a seven. That's two hundred dollars please."
"Damn I wish this was real money."
In the background----"And now the moment you've all been waiting for--tonight's big game winning number. The pot is up to six million, four hundred and fifty two thousand dollars. And tonight's winning numbers are (electronic drum roll) 6…14…25…17…4…and 31."
"J, turn the TV down would you?"
"Sure, hold up. Dump grab them big game tickets out of my jacket, would you?"

Dumpy did as he was told. Once Johnny B looked at the tickets, then at the numbers on the television screen, and then back at his tickets, Dumpy saw an expression on his brother's face which he hadn't seen since they'd discovered that you can brew your own beer. It was an expression of awe, of purpose, and of possibility all rolled into a wide, toothy smile. Well, it wasn't toothy, but that's only because Johnny B lost three teeth in that disastrous fried beak incident at Reba's Poultry Palace (the local equivalent of Water Works on the board).

"Oh my God! Oh my dear sweet Lord Jesus!! Dump come here and look at this, quick before it goes off the TV."
"Holy crap, J, you won."
"**We** won!"
"We're rich."
"OK, simmer down. Take a deep breath and count to six."
"Screw that, we're freaking rich."
"We just won the lottery, Dumpy. Six million dollars. I'm taking us out to steak tonight, brother."
"I say we get a new trailer."

Back at the Harringtons, Ethel was watching Dee's face as she was talking to her husband on the phone about their recent financial windfall. At first Dee's face was in haggard wife mode--(I need to make him get a haircut and cut the lawn). Then her face changed to true mom mode--(I'm a patient woman who can put up with anything). Then it abruptly changed into Holy Crap mode--(My son just made the football team/The stick wasn't really pink/Dear God we just won the lottery).

After five minutes of surprisingly stunted stammering on Dee's part, she hung up the phone and hugged Ethel with all of her might, actually cracking a few joints in the process. Ethel was intrigued.

"What happened, Dee?"

"We, I can't believe this; we just won the lottery...the big one."

"Are you serious?"

"Yeah, unless Johnny B messed up the numbers. But Dumpy's over there and he's good with math."

"Dumpy's good with math?"

"He doesn't have to use his fingers."

"You really just won over six million dollars?"

"I think so."

"So, I guess I better start looking for a new maid, huh?" Ethel said with a wink.

"What? No, I'm not gonna quit you, Miss Ethel."

Diedre Jones is a woman who understands loyalty---common sense, not so much.

"So Dee, are you going to take the lump sum payment or receive the money intermittently through some sort of payment plan?"

"Uh, sure."

"Which one?"

"I don't know. Miss Ethel, I just don't know what I'm going to do. Which one would you do?"

"I don't know."

Ethel Robinson called her lawyer son, Butler, who lives in Atlanta. After an abridged how's-it-going small talk session, she asked his advice.

"Well, what'd he say?"

"He said that you'll actually pay less in taxes with the lump sum, but most of the lump sum people go broke within a few years. It's up to you."

"I can't think about that now. I've got to get the bathtub ready so I can fill it up with hundred dollar bills and roll around in it. Oh, and I want to buy some metal forks. But first, I'm going to bail Sparkles out of jail. It's been two days and we're out of spare breast milk."

"Good call."

CHAPTER SEVEN--CHAMPAGNE DREAMS AND BARBEQUE WISHES

Part One--Diedre Jones

The US mint uses three types of ink to create American currency. Former President Richard Nixon took us off the gold standard, meaning that money is now simply credit, without solid backing. An English colloquialism for money, 'lucre', is most likely a mistranslation from a French word, was used five times in the New Testament, and was popular in WWII era America. None of this mattered to Dee as she rolled around naked in a bathtub full of currency with pictures of Benjamin Franklin's cherubic face. She was as close to heaven as she'd been since her teenaged 'I'm in love for the first time and dreaming of a picket fence and kids and cornbread and ponies' phase. Realizing that she was going to have to water bathe after rolling around in money, Dee was careful...but not too careful to run the sensation gamut with her new found colonial friend. Grabbing huge handfuls of bills, she rubbed them around on her cheeks, smelled them and, for the first time, smelled the smell of freedom and possibility; she finally understood what all those people on TV felt like. After the bath, Dee neatly stacked her bills into twenty little piles. Then she took a water bath, not as emotionally satisfying as a money bath, but it will get you cleaner.

Part Two--Johnny B and Dumpy
The store loomed in the distance like a behemoth, like the standard historical statue centerpiece for the main street areas of many a small Southern town, like something big at the end of something long. The store--Randy's Guns, Ammo and Salad Bar. The salad bar had started out as a joke, but their endive, leaks and blue cheese crumbles have won over even the most skeptical hunter.

Johnny B and his brother, Dumpy, were walking slowly through the aisles of weapons, hunting accessories, ammunition, croutons, and calendars of anorexic platinum blonde girls with abnormally large breasts in camouflage bikinis. This is what heaven would be like if it were run by Ted Nugent. Like kids in a candy store, if the candy could kill you, these two merry weekend hunters traversed the aisles, throwing rifle after rifle into their red, checkered buggy. They grabbed ammo, a new thirty foot high ascending deer stand, vats upon vats of deer piss (it attracts deer and country girls), new boots, night vision goggles, even an impulse grenade or two. And at the checkout line, they could pay. It was glorious. It was Ramboesque. It was, simply put, perfect.

Part Three--Charity
Surrounded by half naked weight lifters in tight acid washed jeans, Charity reclines on her goose down bed of plastic flowers. Skittles fall from the sky and she catches them in her mouth. The ones that miss her mouth are swiftly gathered by the strapping young, mute, men and are then fed to her. She yawns and takes a nap while being massaged roughly.

Part Four--Sparkles and Oh-Oh
Sparkles sat in a flying Lazy-Boy chair as it whirred throughout the mall. She was able to hurl projectiles at the girls who made fun of her in high school, and once the magic concrete balloons hit the girls, they turned ugly. An unsuspecting cheerleader was instantly given tree-trunk legs. A popular hippie girl grew a handlebar mustache. A well-liked Honor Society achiever instantly found that she had the head of a grasshopper. Then Sparkles would look at them, chuckle and fly on to the next unsuspecting shopper. The Limited was full of some ugly, ugly chicks that day.

Oh-Oh was in Vegas. This is a baby with little to no idea of sensory overload. He doesn't even understand the concept. But he likes colored lights, candy available at the touch of a The Cow Says Moo spin toy, and large breasts (although for a different reason than the rest of us). So, Vegas makes sense. Oh-Oh was in a red wagon, but one with rocket boosters, one with the power of teleportation, and one without adult supervision.

Part Five--Hannah
Revenge...sweet revenge...it's a dish best served cold, but that doesn't apply to impulsive mountain women with an axe to grind with their daughters, or, in Hannah's case, an axe to grind against her daughter. The revenge scenarios are too many to enumerate, but one of them involved an ant hill, a Garden Weasel and a two liter of honey...another one involved chains, an angry rhinoceros and a Wiffle bat...and those are just the ones which aren't too disturbing to mention.

Of course those were just money fantasies, what some might call the American dream...what Donald Trump would just call Tuesday... and what the Joneses now call possible.

Back in reality, or as close to reality as suburbia is capable of, Dee and Ethel were talking over sweet tea and biscuits.

"Dee, I'm telling you, don't worry about it, honey. I know you're a worrier, but, besides your mom, most of the stuff you used to worry about dealt with money. Now you're going to have money, and you still look worried."

"I think I'm just a worrier, Ethel. Can't help it. Momma used to scare me everyday, and I know it sounds like I'm at a head shrink's office, but that don't mean it's not true."

"Well, what can I do to help?"

"OK, well Johnny B and me settled on getting the one big payment. I think he just wants to hold the big check."

"Who wouldn't?"

"I know. I do too. It'll just feel, you know, real. I hope. But what I really want to know is what to do with the money once we get it."

"Well, that depends. What are your financial goals?"

"Uh, I want it in the bank."

"Right, but I mean do you want to put it in a low yield but safe money market account, invest in the market, or set up trusts for your kids?"

"Jeez Miss Ethel, I don't know."

"Well, that's what we're here to find out, Dee. The first bit of advice I'd give you Dee, is remember who your friends are, 'cause you're about to see some long lost relatives and old friends coming out of the woodwork."

"Uh-huh."

"But Dee, first off, go out and buy something you've always wanted."

"Like Branson, Missouri."

"Maybe. But I don't think that they generally sell cities, per se. What about something that's actually purchasable?"

"Like them giant inflatable trampolines they got at the fair?"

"Maybe. But that's for Oh-Oh. What about you, what do you want?"

"Well, I've always wanted a maid."

"Perfect."

"Oh and I was thinking that we should buy The Corner, ya know, as like a project for Johnny B and Dumpy. PH's been talking about selling for years."

"Great. They'd love it."

"I've got to call and tell him."

After Johnny B and his wife discussed the possibility of their buying The Corner, he'd let the idea rattle around in his brain before bringing it up with his brother. Johnny B and Dumpy were seated at a strained table in the back of Madame Shaniqua Wong's All You Can Eat Chinese/Soul Food buffet, and the two of them were currently stretching the definition while a worried Madame Wong looked on in horror.

"So, what'cha think, Dump?"

"'Bout owning The Corner? It's great, best idea you've ever had."

Johnny B didn't feel the need to tell his brother that it wasn't actually his idea.

"What could we do with it though?"

"Oh, damn, listen, we could have a waterslide. You know I can't resist a waterslide."

"Or a machine that dispenses beer like gum balls. They could be beer balls, or you could just put your mouth to the hole and suck out the beer."

"Kinda gay, don't you think?"

"OK, then a beer fountain. Or an above ground beer pool? Or what about solid beer? Do they have solid beer, like beer that you chew?"

"No, but there's a reason fer that, JB."

"We need mud wrasslin' and an honest to God stage for music. Now that we've got money, we could even get real bands. Heck we could get Willie. He's still alive, sort of. Or Travis. Shit brother, we can get Alabama."

"And WWE. We could maybe get real wrasslin, get them to come down here for a smack down, not this local face off, same people every week crap."

The preponderance of prodigious possibilities poured out of the portly brothers for hours, which only deepened the worry lines in Madame Wong's face and decimated her chicken wing and spring roll supply. The next week she dropped All You Can Eat from the title.

CHAPTER EIGHT--THE SHAH OF NORTH GEORGIA

The Piggly Wiggly had never shined as brightly as it did on that day. Employees of The Pig were dressed in tuxedos and full length ball gowns, the manager wanting to take advantage of the free publicity that comes along with a press conference held in his parking lot. Watermelons were half off. Powdered donuts were twelve minis for a dollar and a half. Sausage and cheese samples were available on a plate flying through the air at shoulder height, connected to a wrist, which was then connected to an arm, which was then connected to Randy. The samples were only available if you could get to them before Johnny B. After the third plate, Randy had to convince the cute check out girl, Betty Sue, to block for him and flirt with Johnny B so that he could make the rounds.

The large, size of your average European car, black block lettered, not-actual-currency, oversized check was being carried toward the assembled Joneses by the two lottery officials present in the Comment Piggly Wiggly parking lot that day. Peter Reinhold was one of the top lottery guys. He was efficient. He was proper. He was scared shitless of being in Comment, but managed to hide it under a massive layer of human bureaucracy, the likes of which most of us don't see unless we work at the Social Security office. Peter was there with a dual mission: to ensure that this family gets their money and that the lottery system gets good press. He was worried that the Joneses would embarrass the lottery system, and he was right of course, but that doesn't really differentiate them all that much from most lottery winners. Peter was also the man responsible for changing the venue from the Pretty Good Market to the most photogenic location in Comment, Georgia, the Piggly Wiggly Parking lot.

The other lottery official on site was Gregory. Gregory was a sycophant's sycophant. He was voted most likely to kiss ass in high school, partly as a backhanded gay joke, but also because the guy was a born brown-noser. The man had no shame. He was the SS officer who'd ask Hitler to sign his ass while he combed the Fuhrer's tiny mustache. He was the nutritionist who'd tell Keith Richards to keep up the good work. He was the guy who you hated in high school, but couldn't pinpoint exactly why; you just knew that he creeped you out a little in a very polite and unspecified way.

Peter was arranging the cameras and accommodating their lighting and other problems while Gregory's job was to make sure the winners were comfortable enough not to complain about anything on air. They both had their jobs down to a science. Gregory was giving Dee a well-deserved shoulder massage, which normally would've sent Johnny B into a jealous rage, if Gregory's same sex tendencies weren't as obvious as your average drag queen. Gregory was prepping the mater and pater of the Jones family for the brief interview:

"No Mr. Jones. You are of course welcome to say whatever you like. It's a free country. But we at the lottery would prefer if you didn't use any vulgarity."

"Like fucking what?"

"Well sir, like that."

"I know man. Just kiddin'."

"Oh (insert fake laughter here), I get it. You got me Mr. Jones. Ha-ha-ha. Um, also, if there's any way, no forget that. Mr. Jones, why don't you go over and see the make up lady from channel 2, the little blonde girl over there with the eye liner in her hand? She'll fix you up."

"With make-up?" Johnny B looked to his wife, to see if she thought it was too unmasculine to wear make-up, but Dee was in full on massage relaxation mode and didn't care. Gregory just wanted to get rid of him so that he could talk to Dee alone.

"OK, Mrs. Jones. Why don't you do the talking for the family, you know be the spokesperson?"

"You want me to shut my husband up? Good luck."

Johnny B was enjoying being made up, maybe a little too much, which would've worried him, but he just figured that all rich people wore make up.

Finally, after a lengthy, largely unsuccessful, make-up session which resulted in two firings, a greenish rash, and a half eaten tube of lipstick, the Joneses were as camera-friendly as they were likely to get. All three big Atlanta TV stations had cameras on-site, as well as various scattered local and regional news outlets, print, internet and televised. Peter was the man who would be the on camera lottery rep and Gregory was the man carrying the big check. There was a podium set up, although no one could figure out quite why. There was a bouquet of microphones in front of the collective Joneses. Johnny B, Dumpy, his wife Elaine, Dee, Sparkles, her husband Mike, Charity and Oh-Oh were in attendance, all of them continuing to dream their oh-so American dreams.

The Joneses were dressed in their Sunday best, except Charity. Charity, wanting to use her fifteen minutes of fame to attract dates, was wearing a particularly tight tied off white tee-shirt on which she'd recently airbrushed her cell phone number in large, glittered, pink numbers. Sparkles had dressed the baby up in his mini tuxedo that they'd stolen from a formally dressed stuffed animal at the mall and Oh-Oh was currently attempting to chew his way through it.

Peter wanted this to go as smoothly as possible. He began with his standard winner speech:

"Hey folks, I'm Peter Reinhold, Georgia lottery spokesman. I wanted to announce our newest big game winners, the Jones family (pause for applause that doesn't come). The Joneses won the big one just a few days ago here in Comment, Georgia. And here they are behind me. My assistant, Gregory, is bringing the big check over to the winners now. Gregory, why don't you present the check to the family?"

Gregory did as he was told. And then he and Peter backed off to the camera views' periphery and nervously let the Joneses have the spotlight for the standard round of banal questions from the standard, banal reporters.

"Mr. Jones, Omar Washington, channel six, where did you purchase the winning ticket?"

"Uh, well. My brother Dumpy and me was at the Pretty Good Market. Say hey Dump."

Dumpy's wife Elaine was an histrionic woman, a woman prone to exaggeration and not the most trustworthy of people, but she wasn't stupid. She knew why Dumpy went to the Pretty Good Market. She knew about Miss Lola Jane Copeland and her former beauty queen glory. Elaine's eyes widened in angry disbelief as she connected the dots. Standing next to Dumpy, she hit him once in the stomach. He doubled over and then jerked his head up, face toward the cameras, as they both continued to fake smile for the cameras.

"Mr. Jones, Alisha Wallace, channel two, what did you do when you first discovered that you had the winning ticket?"

"Uh, well, me and Dump was playing a board game when the ball picker girl came on TV, the cute one, the colored girl. And then we checked it twice and when we realized that we won, we, uh, we got excited. I think I jumped up and down, but not too hard. The trailer's floor's a little thin you know, but when the colored girl said my..."

Dee leaned over and whispered something inaudible to the cameras into Johnny B's ear.

"Naw, honey, that ain't offensive. Hey, Miss Wallace, you're colored, tell me, is that offensive?"

"Um…yeah." Unusually long, strained silence accompanied by wide-eyed, stunned disbelief.

"Ooookkaay, sooo, Mrs. Jones, what are you planning to do with the money?"

"Well, I want to put a lot of it in the bank. My friend Ethel is going to help me. She's real smart with money. But first, I want to buy a car, a Camaro or maybe a Mustang, something with some giddy-up, or no, let's buy a boat."

Elaine's face was turning redder by the second and she was about to lose bladder control, as she usually does when she's angry, which is often. Unable to contain herself any longer, Elaine let out a mini war cry and dove at her husband, hitting him repeatedly with a barrage of little fists.

"You were flirtin' with Lola Jane. Don't lie to me, you fat tub of shit! That's what you was doing at the Pretty Good. You worthless, fat bastard!"

Dee, sensing that things were coming unraveled, began a camera soliloquy to try and keep the cameras off of the melee.

"Well y'all we've got lots of things we want to buy...like jewelry, and some new hunting gear, maybe a new house, or what'd I say, a boat, maybe one of those swamp boats, maybe a weird pet like a snake or something..."

"You cheating, lying, worthless nothing of a man. Stepping out on me. Did she give you winning ticket? Did she, you fat tub of crap?"

"Elaine, honey. Come on. You know I love you, only you."

Johnny B and Oh-Oh started laughing uncontrollably. Mike and all of the media people stood there in mute, shocked silence. Charity puffed out her breasts and angled for camera space. Sparkles tried in vain to keep Oh-Oh from eating his clothes on television. And a now pee-soaked Elaine continued to beat Dumpy. The number of bleeped 'cuss' words on that broadcast set a new Georgia record and the sheer amount of classic B-role footage collected that day was enough to set the South back twenty years. Lottery officials tried to find a judge who would issue a quick injunction to keep the news outlets from rolling it, but that simply was not going to happen. Once things get momentum, they're hard to stop. And you just can't make up this kind of stuff.

The day after the Piggly Wiggly fiasco, the Joneses received their lump sum, regularly sized check. In the accompanying congratulatory letter, they were told the name of a well-reputed local accountant who could help them with the huge initial tax payment. The lottery doesn't advertise it of course, but you wind up paying a lot in taxes whenever you get one large payout on anything.

Mordecai Berg, CPA, had always loved money. He used to eat it as an infant, which is probably the reason that his taste buds no longer function. Everything tastes like cheese. But, sensory issues aside, he's a whiz with money. Last April, Mordecai saved Big Bob, of Big Bob's Feed store fame, over ten thousand dollars that he thought that he was going to have to give to the damned government. Big Bob has a correspondingly big mouth and now everyone in town thinks that Mr. Berg is a financial genius. This kind of rumor is easy to start due to the fact that, as a concept, giving the government money doesn't go over well in the South.

Since Dee is in awe of all Jews, she all but genuflected when she walked into his sparsely decorated office. After kissing Mr. Berg's mezuzah and sheepishly peeking her head inside the office, Mr. Berg invited Dee and Johnny B inside. They sat and talked about ways to cheat the government.

Although Johnny B did have to write out a sizable check for taxes, it was still the largest check he'd ever written, technically the first check he'd ever written, as the Joneses had been a largely cash family before recent events. Johnny even had to pull the dusty check book out of his hope chest. It was right below the spandex he plans on wearing for his wrasslin' debut, and next to his genuine Creek Indian scalp (which he bought at a flea market and is, let's hope, a used toupee').

Mr. Berg was now the official financial advisor for the Nuevo-riche Joneses. He'd advised them to set up a few trusts, and made a couple of suggestions about possible safe blue chip investments. Next up was a quick trip to the Dairy Queen with congratulatory Blizzards for all. Even Dairy Queen employees frown on a young mother giving her infant son a candy treat with enough calories to satisfy a team of oxen for a week. But having your parenting skills judged by the girl with seven abortions who runs the soft scoop machine is rough, but hard to take seriously. Luckily, the Joneses are immune to that kind of judgment. They didn't care when they were poor and they sure as hell don't care now.

COMMENT HILLBILLIES--No, it's not redundant, you snob
America=new car. New Car=new car smell. New Car Smell=progress.
OK, that's not true, but everyone loves that smell. Even Ralph Nader has to admit that it smells good, though he'd probably insist on a nose belt for the driver.

Diedre Jones was enjoying that new car smell as she, her husband and their two daughters wound through the town...in their new Camaro...looking for their new house. It took the family a few days to realize that since they're now rich, they could buy a house instead of simply upgrading their trailer...but they got there eventually.

The Camaro was jet black with orange racing stripes, kind of like a smaller, sleeker, faster A-team van, which, unfortunately, didn't come equipped with BA Barracus. Johnny B was driving. Dee was navigating by classified ad. Basically they were looking at the houses listed in the classifieds. Everyone at the houses had seen one of the newscasts (channel six showed it on a repeating loop for three days). So, when the black Camaro pulled up, the owners of the house recognized the rubber burning smell of new money----and watching an old money family kiss a newly rich redneck family's ass, now that's a sight to see. The old money family knows that they have to compliment the necks, but it just feels weird saying something complimentary about three inch pink heels or anything remotely camouflage.

SAMPLE DIALOGUE:
"Hey winners. Come on in and check out the house. By the way Mrs. Jones, that's a beautiful tube top you're wearing. Is that Chanel?"
"Uh, Dollar Store."
"Well, it looks lovely on you dear. And you, young lady, those black Army boots go well with your bleached hair."
"Um, thanks. I try."
"And that's a lovely brooch you're wearing my dear."
"That's a mustard stain."

Meanwhile in a plush trailer in Woodland Springs, a mountain woman was complaining to her husband. Hannah had seen the footage of her daughter and her daughter's family, of which she used to consider herself a member. That footage delighted, saddened, and excited Hannah. She was, on one level, angry about her recent banishment from the family. She was also happy that the Joneses had made such fools of themselves on the news, but it still made her sad for her lost familial honor and jealous that she hadn't been there.

Hannah was cooking pork and collards while Nestor, just home from work, was watching fútbol on Univisión, and nursing a Budweiser. In other words, Nestor wasn't listening to his wife, which didn't matter to Hannah anyway, as she was only really looking for a human sounding board to nod occasionally and agree with her. And Nestor had long ago learned how to placate his wife without having to disturb his own routine. It's a truly integral part of marriage.

"All them on the TV, making fools of themselves, and making fools of my family name. My daddy's rollin' over in his grave thinking about that crazy sight."

"Oh yes."

"Still, it woulda been nice to be there. I mean, Dee's barely my daughter anymore, but she's still family."

Uncle P, the family's resident junkie and life-long momma's boy, walked in (if you can't score a free meal from your mother, then it's time to start dumpster diving).

"Hey, ma."

"Hey Peter. Come give momma a hug. You see Dee on TV?"

"Yeah." He laughed subtly. "Funnier than any news I ever seen."

"Jealous?"

"That Johnny B won the lottery, damn right I'm jealous. Hey Nestor, football? Right on. Oh, it's soccer. Why do you Mexicans like that stupid sport so much?"

Nestor, not understanding and truthfully not caring, nodded at Peter. Nestor knew how to shut his son-in-law up. You nod at him in agreement, and, if that doesn't work, you keep a small methamphetamine stash for emergencies (it sounds paradoxical, but once you get him on speed, you push him out the door and he goes looking for more speed--works every time--and truthfully, when you run out of drugs, giving him a large bag of baking powder works almost as well--the mind is a strange, but interesting, place).

"Momma, I'm gonna drink a few with Nes before dinner."

"Don't even try changing the channel. He loves his soccer."

Nestor shrugged. It was his gesture.

HOUSE HUNTING

The house was grand, in every sense of the word. It was big-four stories, huge intimidating front porch to keep away the political canvassers and Jehovah's Witnesses, two-acre back yard, enough working toilets to ensure that everyone gets his or her own bathroom, even a Jacuzzi, which can double as a urinal in a fix. It was also grand in the sense that it produced a sense of grandeur in the viewer. After disemusclecarring from their new Camaro, the Joneses stood in awe, looking at one of the possibilities for their new shelter. They stared for five silent minutes until the couple selling the house came outside and joined them. Like almost everyone in a five county radius, the couple (Robert and Rebecca O'Leary) had seen footage of the Piggly-Wiggly debacle multiple times on multiple channels, and had even caught the hastily-made dramatic recreation on TNT starring teen heartthrob, Bucky Power. Robert and Rebecca's house had been 'listed' for close to three years now. Due to the fact that they were asking a shade less than three hundred thousand for it, interested parties had been few and far between. Keeping your house selling clean for three years is a pain in the butt, and so, by this point, the exasperated O'Learys had all but dropped any sense of honesty or decency from their sales pitch.

"Come on inside, folks. Those are the exact words that the previous owners told Franklin Delano Roosevelt when he came here for lunch."

"Who?"

"FDR. The president..."

No knowing looks of recognition.

"...of football."

"The president of football visited here."

"Sure did, Mr. Jones. But that's not all. It's rumored that during the Civil War, General Sherman was going to burn the house, but he felt the presence of Jesus inside, so he, uh, decided instead to, um, hold a worship service here, with big tents, and, uh, and a water slide."

"A water slide? For real? I love those things. Do you still have it?"

"No, sir. Sadly, it was, um, stolen by Jesse James when he was in the area."

"Jesse James. Honey you hear that?"

Dee, Johnny B and the O'Learys strolled leisurely inside the house. Robert and Rebecca learned two years ago that it's in their best interest to have sweet tea and cookies prepared for potential buyers. They led the Joneses inside, through the shining white front doors, past the foyer, down the long wood paneled front hallway, through the spacious and immaculate den/adult play room, past the viewing window which shows the kids' play room (so wealthy parents can supervise without having to actually touch their kids), and into the sparkling whiteness of the O'Leary's humongous, size of the Jones's entire trailer, fully equipped kitchen. Johnny B and Diedre were both too stunned to speak readily, but after a few cookies, a smattering of small talk, and a fake compliment or two, their respective tongues loosened.

"Mr. O'Leary, tell us, hoss. Why ain't y'all sold this palace before now?"

"Well truthfully, I don't know, Mr. Jones. It's a lovely house, as you can see, but most people just don't have as much money as you two."

We all have our ups and downs. When we get our dream job, publish our first rambling pointless novel, or give birth to our first child, it's a good moment. When we spend our first night in jail, catch our first venereal disease, or get mugged by our first pre-teen, it's a bad moment. When a strange couple referred to the Joneses as rich, it was a good moment. In fact, unbeknownst to the O'Learys, it was the real reason they were finally able to sell their house after three long, grueling years of patience, having their hopes dashed and even attending that 'How to Swindle People in Business, Love, or at a Swap Meet' seminar.

Once they both simultaneously realized not only that they were in fact now rich, but that everyone knew it, the Joneses attempted to hide their smiles, but both felt better than they had since the opening of the new 24 hour Krystal two blocks from their trailer. After their snack, the O'Learys showed the Joneses the remainder of their four tiered house. In total there were fifty rooms. If you've only ever lived in pre-fabricated homes, then touring a mansion is like getting invited to house sit the White House while the president's in Europe. It's shocking, exhilarating, a little scary, completely adrenaline producing, and just straight up weird.

The backyard consisted of an acre of woods, a small, but well-manicured, garden, a man-made pond (stocked with blue gill and small mouth), a two-car garage with a 'barely tolerated guest' room above, a Jacuzzi, and a massive dog run. The house was like a hot stack of buttery pancakes, but the back yard was like the syrup and powdered sugar. Standing on the rear deck, a sturdy, stained wooden contraption, overlooking what was soon-to-be-his kingdom, Johnny B only had one word:

"Damn."

A MEAL FIT FOR A KING...maybe the mattress king, or the king of beers.

Orlando's Catering, Spackling, and Nonsexual Massage Parlor had recently been focusing on the catering aspect of its eclectic business interests. Orlando's chef, Mitzy, was county-renown for her cornbread with actual whole kernels of corn, 'miracle corn prizes', baked inside. As a celebratory meal for the Joneses, Ethel Robinson had ordered the "Full Load" from Orlando. The "Full Load" consists of thirty steaks prepared according to taste, a basket of cornbread, mashed potatoes (lumpy, smooth, or sausaged), barbecued ribs, green beans, Cole slaw, a twelve pack of Orlandonuts (same as regular donuts, but with hot sauce), two cakes of the customer's choosing, water, tea, Coke, or all three. Orlando didn't mess around when it came to catering. His spackling left much to be desired, but that was mainly due to the fact that he used his leftover potatoes as a cost effective alternative to actual spackle. Unfortunately for Orlando, mashed tubers don't hold up as well in the rain as he'd hoped.

Ethel hadn't had the full-on Jones family experience for months. But, everyone except Hannah, Uncle P, Nestor, and the incarcerated Eric, was assembled at the Harrington's that day. For once Dee didn't even have to clean up and set the table, but she did anyway. We're all of us creatures of habit.

Ethel had two maroon picnic tables aligned end to end in her back yard. She covered them with one of those cheap, thin, barely retaining the properties of a solid, kiddy birthday party tablecloths. Then she covered that with Armor All. Then she had Orlando's delivery staff arrange the sumptuous feast on top of that.

Dee, Johnny B, Elaine, Dumpy, Sparkles, Mike, Oh-Oh, Ethel, Charity and her date (a bearded, scraggly, confused local folk singer named Vlad Corneliouson) were all playing with their forks and filling up their glasses, waiting for someone to thank God so they could dive in. Knowing full well that a simple, respectful, humble Episcopal prayer wouldn't be enough to satisfy a Church of Christ Calvary Holiness Baptized Evangelical family, Ethel had asked Dumpy if he'd say grace.

"Bow yer heads everybody, and somebody hold the baby's head down and put their other hand over his mouth to shut him up. OK, dear Lord, first off, thank you for letting Johnny B and Dee win the lottery, and thank you more for the generosity and goodness you gave my brother and his family. Thank you for teaching him that sharing is good, and sharing with your own kin is even better. Thank you for teaching him that it's better to give than to not give your brother any of that lottery money. Thank you for Dee and her love for everyone, especially her own flesh and blood, or the people who ain't her blood but are related by marriage and by that marriage non blood she's married to my brother. Oh, and thanks for the food. AMEN."

"Heck Dump, you don't need to involve The Big Guy. You know I'm gonna hook you up. We're buying the Corner together, you and me, JB and Dump man."

"I know. I know. I'm just nervous, you know. This whole thing's just weird."

"But, Dump, just cause I bought the ticket, don't mean we didn't both win. Oh, hey, Ethel, this looks delicious. Orlando's?"

"Mitzy makes an impressive spread."

"I love these little miracle corn breads, Miss Ethel."

"Thank you, Sparkles, but I didn't cook them so I can't take credit. Everyone, I didn't know how y'all liked your steaks, but I took a chance and guessed that you like them pretty well done. So we've got a medium rare for me and another for whomever. We've got two mediums, and the rest are all well done."

"You know us too well, Miss Ethel. Pass the ketchup."

MOVING DAY

The familiar shape of the medium sized stand alone U-haul truck pulled up into the ritzy neighborhood. As it did, a hush came over the assembled crowd of nosy neighbors and curious onlookers. The neighbors all knew who was coming, and, with hushed whispers and palpable angst, they awaited the Apocalypse which they all believed was an inevitable aspect of a trailer family moving in. They weren't entirely wrong.

You know how when something tragic happens in the middle of Conformerica people just stand around and marvel at it. Sure, sometimes an enterprising young lad will call 911 or give the CPR class refrain, 'Are you all right, are you alright?' But, for the most part, people stand around in a circle, or perhaps a semi-circle, and gawk, or semi-gawk. We're a nation of gawkers--and it's not just THEM, it's US too; it's you, and me. I know you think that you're better than that, but you're not. Anyway, a semi-circular patterned crowd was there to greet the Joneses to the neighborhood. In groups of four or five (two tall, the rest short) they came up and introduced themselves, said their welcomes, and went home to stare through mini blinds from a comfortable distance.

Jones Manor, as it will come to be called, is the second nicest house in the neighborhood. But the house next door was bigger. Jones Manor has an acre of woodland and a below ground pond for a backyard. Johns Palace, the house next door, had two acres of backyard and an above ground pond that's closer to fishing hole than actual lake, but still big. Allen "AJ" Johns was the founder, front man and CEO of Let's Fro Down Records, a rap and R & B outfit based in Atlanta, which had recently put itself on the fast track with Truly Freaking Obese, a creative trio of formerly shut-in sized black guys who rap about finding pork chops and French Fries in their fat rolls, the perils of Slim Fast, and of course sex with skinny Asian girls. America has a taste for bad taste. Allen Johns was taking out his garbage in preparation for the following morning's pick up service, when he spotted the Joneses in the midst of their moving day. Johnny B locked eyes with Allen and the two warily approached each other like two dogs circling each other out at the park, preparing to sniff.

"Hey, Allen Johns. I'm your neighbor. Saw y'all on the news. You really call us all colored?"

A moment of stunted possibility passed in a mental Mexican standoff, ironically since neither man likes Mexicans.

"Yeah, sorry. I thought that was what I's supposed to say."

Uncomfortable pause...

"Funniest fucking thing I've seen on TV in a while. Of course you realize it's offensive as hell."

"Yeah, I didn't mean nothin', just what my momma said."

"But it ain't fair, you know. My momma called white folks 'crackers', but it just doesn't have the oomph to piss white people off these days... I'm working on some new ones."

They both started laughing and shook hands, made fake plans, and said a lot of nothing. Johnny invited Allen to have a beer while the women stood around telling burly, sweaty, Latino mover men where to put their stuff. It's the new American class system in action.

The majority of the Jones' stuff was still largely incongruent with their new accommodations. Sure they'd only recently purchased the life-sized animatronic Nativity scene, but wealth alone doesn't mean that the old money folks were going to tolerate crap like that. However, Allen Johns, with his suped-up Bentley, equally Nuevo-riche attitude and life-sized wax Huey Newton mock up lawn ornament couldn't care less.

The Joneses had met the neighbors.

CHAPTER NINE--GENTLEMEN CALLERS

[[Capitalism--*Brit*--n--1877--an economic system characterized by private or corporate ownership of goods, by investments that are determined by private decision, and by prices, production, and the distribution of goods that are determined mainly by competition in the free market.]] That's Webster's take on it. Still they might want to add a little addendum saying that if you come into a large amount of money in a short period of time, you are going to be assailed by a large and varied group of opportunistic fucks who are only there to take your money...and some of them are family. It's pretty much immutable fact.

First came Nestor. Dee and Johnny B like Nestor. It took a while, but they do. Believe it or not, Nestor's calming influence has tempered Hannah's anger a little. And so, when Nestor came by and sheepishly asked Johnny B for enough money to buy the world's largest van (as a part of his secret plan to slowly bring his entire family up to El Norte from Chiapas now that they're rich), he didn't leave disappointed. And it made Johnny B feel good to begin to make some inroads into reuniting mother and daughter.

Next up was the agent. A "talent" agent sauntered up to Jones Manor and after introducing himself and agreeing to come inside for leftover sweet tea and cookies, he began pitching the idea of the family's needing an agent to each and every Jones he could find. When Dee asked Dale McGivern, super agent, why they needed his services, he said that she was going to need someone to take care of booking her on Oprah. When Johnny B asked the same question, Dale said that when Guns and Ammo Magazine wants an interview, they're going to need to talk to some one with experience. When Charity asked, he said that guest VJ spots on MTV don't book themselves. Dale knew what he was doing. He even tried to kiss the baby, but gave up when Oh-Oh refused to stop gnawing on his nose. And just like that, the Joneses had an agent. None of them actually knew why, but now it's done.

Dee swears that she saw the agent hi-five the financial advisor when they passed at the door. The financial advisor didn't fare as well as the agent, since the family was now firmly convinced that Mordecai Berg was a monetary god. That and the fact that the advisor was Mormon meant that he didn't last five minutes in Jones Manor. Honestly, no one wants a Mormon CPA.

Charity's lifelong push for a more intense social life was now reaching its zenith. She'd always been popular with the boys, but now she was 'tomboy supermodel with a prosthetic Playstation arm, a weed dispenser for an ear, and a reputation for giving blow jobs in line at the post office' popular. Boys she'd known in high school, boys she'd known of in high school, the employees at Rita's restaurant, her old guidance counselor, her exes, they all started pummeling her with calls. In retrospect, even Charity admits that putting her cell number on TV was a mistake. But damn did she love the attention. Two former crushes of hers both practically begged her to go out with them. In her head she said no as a form of long suppressed revenge; in reality, she had some sex. Dee warned her that these boys were obviously just gold-diggers, even going so far as to reference the brief period when cousin Jenny was popular because, due to a deep fryer incident at Reba's Poultry Palace, she received free chicken gizzards for a year.

The strangest gentleman caller was a pedestrian environmental canvasser who knocked on the door with his clipboard, his white boy dreadlocks, his optimistically angry sense of what's wrong with the world, and his brochure bag. Environmental canvassing is a weird thing in America to begin with, in the South even more so, and in a *nouvo-riche* mansion populated by a bright red family of recent lottery winners who's previous concern for the environment involved not dumping the used Freon directly into the river, it's beyond weird.

"Hello. My name is Brian. I'm with the Georgia Forrest Defense Fund. We're in your neighborhood talking to people about how developers are destroying our once pristine woodland in order to make room for mini malls and yogurt bars."

"There's gonna be a yogurt bar? Aww, I love yogurt. What kind of toppings?"

"Uh, sir, I think you might've missed the point. I'm out here tonight collecting money and signatures on this petition to try and stop K and K developers from clear-cutting that patch of formerly untouched woodland just two miles east of you. It's near our communal drinking water source which will undoubtedly get polluted and furthermore..."

"Wait, which way's East there, hippie boy? I don't have my compass on me. But hey, sun's still out. Make like you're one of those, what're they called old timey clocks?"

"Uh, a sundial?"

"That's it. Go out and stand in the yard. Good. Now raise one hand up and point it toward the sun. Good, good. Now put your other arm straight out. There you go. Now spin around. No, spin faster. Good, good. Now get the fuck out of my yard, hippie."

Johnny B had just discovered one of the true perks of money in America: it's so much easier to humiliate people. Granted it's not hard to humiliate hippies in the Deep South, but now the Joneses can mess with anybody with impunity. Nowhere in God's plan does it say to let Johnny B Jones discover that eighty-seven point four percent of Americans are willing to humiliate themselves for money. He discovered it anyway.

But, that didn't seem to bother Johnny B when he made the one-armed homeless guy crab walk across the street for a dollar, or when he forced the political canvasser to say his little spiel while funneling Nightrain, or even when he told the telemarketers that he only gave money to people who speak fluent Pig-Latin. Johnny B Jones was enjoying his fellow man more and more.

Later that afternoon at the Harringtons, Dee was explaining to Ethel the perks and burdens of being lottery winners over iced coffee and miniature muffins (we'll call them mini-muffins).

"And then something like five preachers came by. You know me,

Miss Ethel, I don't want to make the Lord mad or nothing, but, those guys seemed more interested in our money than our souls. I mean, they never came around before."

Ethel had to physically restrain herself from giving out a loud and proud "I told you so". She just nodded in semi-motherly sympathy.

"And it weren't just the preachers neither. There was an agent, a money guy, a bodyguard, and a guy who looked like a terrorist. I mean, he said that he was selling magazine subscriptions, but he was wearing one of those do-rags and the big necklaces, and he looked Arabish, so we're pretty sure he was a terrorist. The cops didn't think so when they got there and Dumpy untied the guy."

Suppressing a gasp/laugh, Ethel asked, "Did y'all hire any of them?"

"The agent and the bodyguard, yes, but that's it. You never know. We might need an agent and it couldn't hurt having some muscle around the house."

Although Ethel couldn't conceive of anyone not being scared off by Johnny B and Dumpy's combined girth, she had to admit that an excess of muscle probably wasn't the main reason they were both big.

"What's the bodyguard like?"

"He's big, really big and he used to play pro football until he hurt his knees. We tested him out."

"Do you mean that you had him beat somebody up?"

"No, no, but maybe we should. We just wanted to see if he had that get out of here bodyguard stare at you thing down...and he does."

"I guess that would be important."

"Oh Lordy, I almost forgot to wash the clothes."

Ethel shook her head in disbelief.

CHAPTER TEN--OLD HABITS, CRIME BOSSES AND DUMPY'S OFF BROADWAY DEBUT

The Corner was in the process of rebirth--it was getting a makeover--it was politely resolving its midlife crisis--it was in the middle of changing from an authentic country dive bar to an authentic country dive bar with more stuff. It's as if, say a guy has been a garbage man all his life and in his mid 50's he diversifies and starts giving poetry readings, opens a tattoo parlor for hemophiliacs and paints his hair blue, but still picks up the garbage. That's what's happening to the Corner.

Johnny B, Dumpy, and PH were sitting in the one old table left in the place. They were sharing a pitcher of Coors Light and directing their "staff" on where to set up the new tables, the new bar games, and the new decor for the latest incarnation of the Corner.

"Y'all going to keep the name, Dumpy?"

"What, the Corner? Of course. It's tradition, PH. We don't want to scare off the regulars."

"But you two <u>are</u> the regulars."

"And we don't want to scare ourselves off. See how that works. Hey, Billy, put the Pop-a-shot in the corner next to the bathrooms and the dart board over there so maybe nobody'll lose an eye."

Billy, the bartender/janitor/bar back/dish washer (honorary title since there are no dishes) /host/only remaining employee, was working with the furniture moving crew which Johnny B had hired on for another week (after they'd quickly finished moving the Jones' stuff out of Paradise Valley and into their new neighborhood--which was officially nameless but the locals called it Pill Hill, due to the abundance of doctors, pharmacists, and bored housewife pill poppers who live there).

Billy is a little man and, like many little men, has the all-too-common 'little man syndrome'. In case you don't have any minute friends or family, 'little man syndrome' can often lead small-statured men into picking fights with large people, snarling at carnies, breaking in line at seafood buffets, and running for president. Billy didn't want to pick a fight with his two new, large bosses, but he still threw them a snarl or two.

"Hey Billy, set them chairs up now over around where the stage's gonna be."

Under his breath, in a failed attempt at sarcasm, "I'll set up your chairs". And then Billy set up the chairs.

"Y'all are really gonna do this sing off thing?"

"Well sure, PH. Makes sense when you think about it. People like singing. More important, girls like singing. When was the last time you had like more than two girls in here on one night?"

"Musta been five years ago or, no, maybe seven, no, never. Never had more than two, and one was always toothless Doris of course."

"Don't say it, Dump."

"You really think people'll come for this?"

"Yeah, hell we advertised in the paper and on the radio. Didn't we, Dump? Dump? Snap out of it, brother."

It took Billy and the movers another half an hour to get the stage, the sound system, the karaoke machine, and the chairs arranged to the liking of Johnny B and his brother. Just as Dumpy was making his third attempt to climb on stage and test out the acoustics, a strange man walked in. He was the best dressed person to have ever entered the Corner on purpose: wearing a pin striped grey tailored Armani suit, polished Italian leather shoes, and more than a few gold accessories. His complexion was olive colored, like a fading house plant leaf. He had a well maintained black goatee, small rectangular sunglasses propped up onto his hair, which looked to be held in place by some sort of gypsy magic, or perhaps hair gel. He walked in, scoped the place out for a minute and then headed toward the three seated men.

"Hey, fella. We're not really open tonight, but I'll get cha something. What's your poison?"

"Rum and Coke. Thanks…I'm Wilkes."

They all shook hands as PH perfunctorily poured a bottom shelf rum and President's Choice Cola for Wilkes, who pulled up a chair and joined them at the table.

"So, Wilkes, uh, you're the first customer we've had since we bought the place. What' cha think?"

"It's nice, like the Rotary Club. I've got to be honest. I'm not here to drink. I'm a businessman and I saw you guys winning the lottery. That's why I'm here, to offer you two a few exciting business opportunities."

Johnny B and Dumpy have already developed **the** central have-money trait: the desire to keep it. This desire usually manifests itself as healthy skepticism, but is often mistaken for aloofness or simply being an asshole, not that there's no cross-over.

"Uh-huh."

"Hey, man, all kinds of folks been comin' round and offering all kinds of stuff. You're not the first."

"Maybe not, but I'm the best. Down here I own five restaurants, a convenience store, two hardware stores, and a few more things I can't remember."

"Uh-huh."

PH was absent mindedly wiping down the bar and eyeing Wilkes suspiciously.

"Well, Wilkes, what are you selling?"

"Basically the chance to stay rich. You guys know how so many lottery winners go broke just a few months after they win? Well, I can keep that from happening to you two. I've got a few ideas for investments. I've been thinking about buying a NASCAR team. Do you two guys know anything about NASCAR?"

It's like if, in the middle of a monotonous college lecture about Jungian archetypes, the professor mentions that he once had anal sex with a dingo, or the look on prison inmates' faces when the warden announces his new prisoners got out of jail for an afternoon every Tuesday program--Johnny B and Dumpy's eyes both widened. Still, not wanting to appear too eager, both of them tried to look calm, but, as always, the eyes are the windows to the soul. And these guys' souls both have pit crews.

"Yeah, we know a thing or two. I guess you're not from around here?"

"No, The Bronx originally, but I've lived all over: Chicago, L.A., Baltimore, Mexico City for a little bit."

"Sounds fun."

"Not bad, but I'm in Atlanta now. Here, give me that card back and I'll write down the address of my headquarters. It's a restaurant. I'm there most of the time. Just drop by and we'll talk about how you two can stay rich and have enough left over so your kids never have to work a day in their lives."

"Well, they ain't worked yet. Why start now?"

After Wilkes faked a laugh and shook both of their large, calloused hands, he hurriedly left. Once they all heard his car driving out of the gravel lot (they plan on paving), PH returned to the table with a Silver Bullet pitcher refill (in the 80's or maybe the 90's Coors Light had a poorly planned, and unfortunately memorable, ad campaign whose slogan was--"The Silver Bullet won't slow you down"--someone sued them for false advertising and won since, technically, yeah, the silver bullet will slow you down--just another one of those God Bless America kind of moments).

"That guy. I know him."

"That Wilkes guy?"

"Yeah. He's in the mob."

"Naw, for real. He can't be a gangster, he's white."

"Most of them are."

"But he dresses so nice."

"Most of them do."

"I'm not so sure, PH. How do ya know?"

"Just trust me, boys. Y'all don't want to get mixed up with that som'bitch."

THE RAID

Webster's Dictionary defines the word 'berserk' as: an ancient Scandinavian warrior frenzied in battle and held to be invulnerable,

OR one whose actions are recklessly defiant. If you read X-Men comics you'll know that Wolverine often entered a berserker state and subsequently kicked serious ass. If you've ever seen a cornered dying animal, it's the same thing. And if you saw Hannah in Jones Manor defiantly tearing up the furniture with a wild, crazed, unfocused look in her eyes, then you'd be hard pressed to say that she wasn't berserk.

It started small and then it grew. Hannah got a tentative 'I'm sorry' Hallmark card from Dee. It was an apology, but Dee hedged a little, since, though she did want to mend fences with her mother, she didn't want to admit guilt when she felt very little. Anyway, Hannah read the card at home and at first gave a "Huh", then the "Huh" became a "Harrumph" (actually a "Bitchumph" which is the American translation of the British "Harrumph"), then the "Bitchumph" crystallized into a "That Little Bitch", which then became a "Who does she think she is?" and quickly morphed into an "I'll show her" which, as it often does, then became an "I'll show everybody". And then it was just a matter of time…specifically the fifteen minute drive from Paradise Valley to Pill Hill.

Once Hannah had shoulder rammed the front door open, Marine-style, and had seen the relative opulence of her daughter's new home compared to even the nicest trailer park in town, she subconsciously realized that she and her daughter had now, on some important level, switched roles (like in an 80's movie where the mother becomes the daughter and the daughter the mother---like that, only with less make-up and better dialogue). Consciously, Hannah was just pissed off… and this from a woman whose fall back emotion is wild-eyed anger anyway.

Dee and Johnny B walked in the front door in defensive positions. They'd noticed the door hanging off its hinges. They'd seen sections of the overturned plush cream colored sectional couch on the front lawn. Dee was worried; that's *her* fall back emotion. Johnny B was in full on ass-kickin' redneck mode, not his fall back emotion, but one which he enjoyed.

As they nervously and cautiously ventured inside their new home, Dee and Johnny B slowly reached the kitchen where they saw Hannah repeatedly stabbing one of Oh-Oh's stuffed animals with a butcher knife. The unlucky toy had started the day off as a giraffe, but now looked more like road kill. Years later Dee would sew the collected remains of Geri the Giraffe into an amalgam animal in order to teach Oh-Oh the dangers of home surgery, but only after they'd caught him involved in an amateur colonoscopy with his neighbor, Anna Beth.

Hannah didn't even slow down when her nervous daughter and angry son-in-law entered. Once finished with the former giraffe, she moved on to the appliances. Hurling the blender across the room and hearing it shatter shocked Dee and Johnny B out of their stunned, frozen stupor. They'd been rubbernecking in silent disbelief, but the crashing sound jolted them into action. Dee sprinted upstairs and called 911, while Johnny B grabbed Hannah around her waist and tried to calm her down. It didn't work. Years of difficult manual labor had hardened Hannah into a muscular force, for a sixty year old woman, and even Johnny B couldn't hold her for long. Once she'd broken free, Hannah leapt at the toaster and she and Johnny B silently watched as it sailed through the sliding glass doors and into the backyard.

The police arrived on the scene in thirty minutes, a Comment 911 record time. After loudly announcing their presence, two local police officers cautiously (re: guns drawn) stepped inside Jones Manor. It took Officer Eckstein and Sergeant Peterson ten minutes to subdue Hannah. And, in that ten minutes Hannah's clearly addled brain must have formed a plan. As the police looked on, she was attempting to goad Johnny B into hitting her.

"Come on, you woman. You're a God-awful husband and your kids are ugly. You're a loser, Johnny. Face it. I wish my daughter had married that Sam Peters guy with the one nostril, even he was better looking than you, you fat piece of junk. Hit me!"

Johnny B wasn't naive enough not to understand the ridiculously obvious plan in Hannah's addled brain. The cops had a quick rubbernecking moment themselves. They're only human, if that, and humans like to watch people fight. Shaking out of it, the policemen did quickly subdue Hannah using the time-honored common method: grabbing one arm and pulling it up behind the perp's back until it hurts, then forcing her to the ground to put on the cuffs. It's rough, but effective.

After the action was over, Sergeant Peterson talked to Johnny B and

Keeping Away From The Joneses

Dee for a few minutes while Officer Eckstein put Hannah in the back of the cop car. As she was being dragged out, Hannah was still yelling uncomplimentary things about Dee, her children, her lack of culinary skill, her status as a street walker, and whatever other insult she could think of at the time.

"Hey, thanks a lot for that officer, uh, Officer Peterson."

"No problem. Are you two going to be pressing charges?"

"What'd the charge be?"

"Well, aggravated assault, destruction of property, breaking and entering, making terroristic threats, you name it."

Officer Eckstein reentered the house just as Johnny B turned to his wife. This was her call.

"I just don't know. I don't want her coming back, but if I press charges then I prob'ly ruin any chance of making up with momma."

"We'll hold her overnight and why don't you call us in the morning?"

"Sure thing. Thanks again officer."

It was then that Dee noticed Officer Eckstein's nametag and, sensing a Jewish presence, promptly dropped to one knee, grabbed his hand and kissed his college ring. She was planning on sacrificing a fattened calf to him, but he left too quickly.

"Well, that was weird."

"Just a matter of time, honey. She's been building up since even before we won."

THE CORNER'S REBUT :

COME ONE

COME ALL

COME TO THE NEW CORNER THIS FRIDAY NIGHT FOR:

COMMENT CATCH A STAR THAT'S RISING UP TOWARD

HEAVEN

The crowd was even bigger than they'd expected. Although the brotherly team of Johnny B and Dumpy had blanketed the town with advertisement, it's usually not easy to break people out of their little routines. Consequently, the boys didn't expect the crowd to be what it was. But, upon arriving, they had to park the new Camaro in Mitchell's body shop parking lot two stores over; The Corner was that full.

This was the debut of the NEW CORNER--the venue for tonight--warm up animal fight acts and then the main event, the sing off. In keeping with what our unquestioned lord and master, TV, has told us is appropriate, three local semi-celebrity judges had been assembled into a panel (it just means they sit behind a table and is not, unfortunately, an acrobatic feat involving the Transformers or furniture mime). Minnie Isringhousen, or Miss Minnie, was a local radio personality for fifty years, and though she recently retired to spend more time with her collard green sculpture, she's still a big fish in a small pond. Jack "Big J" Murphy was a retired pro football player (01-03 seasons as back up right offensive tackle for the Arizona Cardinals). And, Alisha Wallace of channel two news fame had gotten over the fact that the Joneses were kind of naively racist, and had agreed to bury the hatchet and be a celebrity judge...once the check cleared.

As the new, excited to the point of almost wetting their pants, co-owners entered their bar, they saw something wonderful. All of the chairs were full--there were women here, lots of them, and some of them were even good looking--there were people here who never would've set foot in here before for fear of gingivitis or relivinghighschoolgloryasanathlete's foot (common Southern disease, trust me). There was classic country music in the background from their newly installed juke box. People were ordering drinks left and right. Poor PH at the bar looked so overworked and decrepit that Johnny B joined him behind the bar for a while. Dumpy checked on the contestants to see if they were comfortable back stage. Since this was the first night, the boys thought it best to only have a few contestants for fear of not having enough applicants, but, in reality, they had far too many applicants and were forced to whittle the list down to ten "finalists". The audience didn't have to know that the preliminaries didn't exist.

The Warm-Up/Get the people in the mood/get the adrenaline racing idea was animal fighting--you know a variation on the popular world-wide theme of cock fighting, but not limited to genitally euphemistic animals. Animal fighting is technically illegal, probably immoral, and a hell of a lot of fun. Dump had been a little worried that singing and animal fighting would attract such radically different crowds that either half the audience would leave post-animal fight or half would be so disgusted with the idea of animal fights that they'd be grossed out and leave pre-singing. Luckily for the boys, PETA hasn't exactly made too many inroads into Comment, Georgia. In fact the one self-described animal rights activist in Comment was actually a door-to-door sausage salesman with a guilty conscience. The folks all gathered in their chairs to watch the fights through the translucent plastic cage which can be easily wheeled on and off the stage.

First up there was an opossum versus a bobcat. It was even more one-sided than most human vs. human warm up bouts before heavyweight boxing matches. The opossum did what opossums do--it played dead--and the bobcat batted it around a little, flipped it onto its back and simply tore that unlucky marsupial up. It was just bloody enough to get the crowd going. Next, a Rottweiler matched its ferocity against a monkey with a screwdriver. Although the odds were 3:2 in favor of the dog, that was one dirty little monkey. The monkey not only stabbed the Rottweiler to death and seemed to thoroughly enjoy it, but then proceeded to vamp for the crowd. Johnny B made a mental note to buy that monkey or trade one of his daughters for him if possible. There was going to be a snake versus house cat final match, but the snake got a jump on the competition in the green room. Instead, PH led the monkey on a victory lap around the bar (once he'd wrestled the screwdriver out of its hands and given him a congratulatory cigarette) for a chance to low-five bar patrons and take bows. Four locals tried to buy the monkey a drink, but both Dumpy and Johnny B thought that an angry drunk monkey was a sign of the Apocalypse, so they wisely nixed that idea.

After the fights there was a ten minute break to encourage more drinking and allow time for the cage and scattered animal intestines to be cleaned up. Then Johnny B got on stage and announced the celebrity judges. The crowd ate it up. Everyone in Comment loves Miss Millie and Big J. And Alisha Wallace, since she's on TV every night, is like the cousin who eats dinner at your house every night, so now she's more like a sibling. As the only black person present in the middle of a crowd of riled-up country white folks, Alisha did have one of those impossible-to-get-rid-of, back-of-the-mind, 'they-might-kill-me' thoughts, but she was a TV reporter, so she knew how not to let it show. Sure, America has made much of white people being afraid of black people, but that phenomenon works in reverse too, and, thankfully, is on the decline anyway now that all American kids want to be black.

HERE'S THE DEAL--It's pure Star Search/Pop Idol/American Idol/Canadian Idol (all yodeling all the time) rip-off. Much like the Gobots or current women's fashion, the Comment Catch a Star That's On the Way Up To Heaven Competition's very unoriginality is what makes it popular. The ten 'finalists' were to individually take the stage, sing their song and do whatever dance moves/gesticulation/choreographed clogging they feel would best add to the experience. Then the judges will each fire off a comment: positive, negative or somewhere in-between. Then Johnny B or Dumpy will ask the crowd to applaud and register the collective enthusiasm on their Clapometer (cheaply bought on EBay for twenty-nine ninety five or the bartering equivalent in used socks). PH will register the applause, 1 to 100, on the giant chalkboard behind the bar. And the winner will, obviously, be the contestant who gets the most applause. First place prize=private audition with a music agent from Atlanta (whom they pre-bribed for the good press it'll bring). Second place prize=$150 gift certificate at either Big Bob's Feed Store or Madame Rita's House of Pretty. Third place prize=Free drinks at the Corner for a month. Fourth through tenth places each receive an optional back massage from Dumpy (unannounced since Elaine was in the front row beaming with pride at her husband's fifteen minutes of you know).

    The crowd noise was registering at 7 on the Clapometer until Johnny B crawled onstage (with the help of Big J and three others) and approached the microphone. The noise quieted to between a 2 and a 3 as he pulled the mike out of the stand.

    "Hey, folks. How's it going?"

    There was applause and Johnny B had a rock star moment. Everyone needs a few of those in a lifetime.

"All right. All right. Good to see so many of you out tonight. And, damn, look at the all ladies here. Y'all look great. I mean, really, really hot. I'd go on, but my wife's right there in the back. Say hey to my wife, Diedre, everybody."

Dee's cheeks visibly blushed as the 'spotlight' (more commonly known as 'adjustable lamp') moved to showcase her reddened cheeks.

After Johnny introduced the celebrity judges and announced half price gin drinks, he introduced the first singer and scooted off the stage.

"First up, everybody put yer hands together for Irene Douglas singing the classic Dolly Parton number "I Will Always Love You."

Irene Douglas was a shining example of what happens when you don't beat your kids--they grow up and think they're special. The lesson here: smack your kids around a little--you'll feel guilty, but they'll thank you for it later.

Irene was awful, not in a 'voice crack-can't hit the high notes of this very difficult song' way, but in more of a 'what the hell was she thinking-is this a joke' way.

Miss Minnie--Um sweetie, maybe singing isn't your thing?

Big J--She's being nice. You suck.

Alisha--I admire you for trying, but next time, choose an easier song.

Irene tried to hold back the tears as she saw the Clapometer gingerly rise to 15. Back stage she sobbed while Harold "Hal" Parker got onstage with an acoustic guitar. Hal did an unplugged version of Twisted Sister's classic "You're Gonna Burn in Hell". It wasn't that he was particularly good at either playing or singing, although he was. It was more that he was just fun. Parker, the former bass player for the now defunct Alba, Georgia band--Yet Another Gang of Dirty Beatniks, got the crowd into it. The owners smiled at the crowds' enthusiasm and at the miraculous method of unloading surplus moonshine by simply calling it gin.

Miss Minnie--I don't approve of your song, but you're pretty good son.

Big J--I love Twisted Sister, man. Good call.

Alisha Wallace--Not great; not bad, but you've got potential.

Hal registered a 57 on the Clapometer.

Third up was bluegrass picker Jimmy Joe (real name Robert F. Kinsington III). His Foggy Mountain Breakdown rendition, while trite, was just what the doctor ordered, if the doctor is a North Georgia neck drunk on shine. The boy could pick and the comments were all positive. Jimmy Joe got a 62.

Fourth was Trina Hendricks who scored big with her wise choice of "That's the Night the Lights Went Out in Georgia". The panel loved her and the crowd gave her a nearly unbeatable 86. The fifth act was Comment high school seventh year senior, Phil Clinton, who performed an extemporaneous freestyle rap act. Phil rapped about what the audience looked like, which females present he'd like to fornicate with, and how he would go about it, should the situation arise. Unfortunately, Phil had massively misjudged his audience, as evidenced by the total silence greeting him as he finished. He wasn't booed or jeered in any way, but the metaphorical crickets were just a'chirping away. Dumpy had thought to order a few tumbleweeds from Texascrap.com. And the mood lightened a bit when he threw one on stage and it rolled past a stunned Phil.

Miss Minnie--Um, well, that was, uh, different.

Big J--know your freaking audience, kid.

Alisha--As the sole representative of the black community here tonight I've got to recommend that you work on your jump shot (that got a polite, nervous PC fake laugh from the crowd and Alisha had her 'when in Rome' moment for the night).

Phil scored even lower than Irene, which allowed Irene to feel less bad about herself, and she stopped crying long enough to "console" Phil.

Up next was a fortyish platinum blonde woman in her third trimester named Claire who sang the Patsy Cline ditty, "Crazy". That lady could sing. Her comments were completely positive and she got an 88, giving her the lead.

Seventh was folk singer and former Charity paramour, Vlad Corneliouson. Vlad was one of those people who desperately wants to be a singing activist, but is, in fact, too stupid to realize that what he's taking a stand against is harmless. His original song, "Douche' Is From the Devil" was more confusing than inspirational.

Miss Minnie--Um, was that song about what I think it was about?

Vlad--yes ma'am.

Miss Minnie---In that case, it was awful.

Big J--Just horrible.

Alisha Wallace--Yeah, just bad. I mean, the part about vinegar and water as the satanic equivalent of biscuits and gravy was almost clever, no, not even that. You're just bad.

The crowd echoed the judges' sentiment and poor Vlad registered a 10, which did lead Irene once again to stop crying and start drinking, but otherwise had no positive effects whatsoever.

Eighth was going to be the ever popular Miss Lola Jane Copeland from the Pretty Good Market, but Dumpy wisely told her to wait for the next competition and bought her a gilded macaroni necklace, all in an effort to avoid pissing off Elaine. It was a good move. Instead, the eighth spot was given to Patricia Landry, who sang a heartfelt but off-key version of Garth Brookes' "The River". The judges politely panned her and she got a 37 on the Clapometer. Ninth was Mr. Tibbs, long-time Comment High School biology teacher who's rumored to have slept with a girl in each graduating class since 1987. Mr. Tibbs was in a few bands in his twenties and, like most failed musicians, now taught high school. His rendition of Confederate Railroad's incredible ode to classlessness, "Trashy Women" was darn good. The crowd ate it up. I mean, let's be honest, who doesn't like their women just a little on the trashy side?

Miss Minnie--that was funny and you're good.

Alisha Wallace--I agree, that was fun. And you can play.

Big J--Dude, I had you for biology.

Mr. Tibbs--I remember. I failed you, didn't I?

Big J--Well no, it was mainly my fault.

Mr. Tibbs--No, Big J, it was <u>all</u> your fault.

The crowd enjoyed the banter and rewarded him with a 90. He even had to come back onstage and take a mini bow. Mr. Tibbs hadn't felt this good in years. Actually, that's not true, but if you take statutory rape out of the equation, then yeah.

Tibbs should've gone on last, but that's not how things worked out. The tenth and final spot was occupied by Gerald Purkowski who gave the crowd a blast from the past that was actually a little too far into the past for them, signing a collection of death-related nursery rhymes (they're all about death; listen to the words sometime; there's some sick shit in those rhymes--farmer's wives mutilating handicapped mice, odes to the black plague—and these are the things that we teach our kids). The crowd wasn't sure if it was real--it was that surreal.

Alisha Wallace--Was that supposed to be music?

Big J--kindergartens, that's your crowd, man.

Miss Minnie--I'm going to have to agree with Big J here. That was just weird.

The crowd gave him a 12.

After Billy had removed the Clapometer, swept the stage, and mumbled to himself the various detailed methods he'd employ to kill his two bosses, Johnny B crawled back on stage. And once Billy, PH, and two unlucky patrons in the front row helped him to his feet, Johnny B grabbed the mike.

"OK, how about a round of applause for all of our contestants, except that guy who sang about the douche'? What was that mo-ron thinking? Well, y'all, we've got the results. Third place goes to...drum roll?...come on, no drum roll?...why the hell didn't we get a damn drum...OK, y'all give us a fake drum roll."

When someone with a microphone speaks, people generally do what they say. And the mock drum roll/bang on the metal chairs thing sounded pretty good.

"Third place goes to...Trina Hendricks. Come on out here Trina. You win free drinks here for a month, and if you don't want that as a prize, well too bad. Naw, if you don't want it, I'm sure you could sell it to someone in the audience. Congratulations and all that. Once more for Trina. OK, this was tight between first and second place, I mean real close. Second place goes to...I'm pausing for another drum roll y'all, come on...try again, second place goes to...Claire Wiggins for her amazing Patsy Cline impression, you sounded just like her too. Claire, come on out here. Come on folks, she's good and 'bout ready to pop. Clap for Claire."

Claire emerged to applause. Her jean shorts and tight pregnant belly exposing tee-shirt certainly didn't hurt her chances, but she was actually a genuinely good singer and did sound much like the tragic Ms. Cline.

"Claire, you win a gift certificate from Madame Rita's House of

Pretty, not that you need help, mmm. And first place, I guess you know who that is now. Everybody knows this guy. Singing Confederate Railroad's 'Trashy Women' and doin' it justice, was Mr. Bertram Tibbs, or if you ever took biology, Mr. Tibbs. Get yer ass out here, Mr. T."

Mr. Tibbs reemerged from 'backstage' to rampant applause. Since most good teachers are half entertainer anyway, Tibbs knew how to vamp for the crowd. Pulling out some old school wrasslin' 'excite the audience by teasing them' moves, he kept the applause going for a rolling five minutes. He was going to be given a second chance to make a first impression in the music world when he auditioned for talent scout, Reggie Dwight, next week in Atlanta. This was a moment he'd been dreaming of since his high school realization that he was never going to be large enough or enough of a strategic thinker to follow his first love, Sumo chess.

The crowd did eventually file out, leaving the Corner a mess, but a profitable one. The brothers had raked in five grand that night minus expenses.

"What cha say, Dumpy?"

"We done good JB. PH says we got five grand."

"Not bad and next time we won't need the super cheap drink specials so we'll really rack up."

While mopping the stage, "What about charging for parking?"

"Naw, that's just annoying. Plus paying money to rent a space, who does that?"

"Uh, everyone who don't own a house."

"Oh yeah."

Stacking up the folding chairs, "Hey, you wanna go and meet that gangster looking guy tomorrow in Atlanta?"

"What's the worst that could happen?"

CHAPTER ELEVEN---THE WORST THAT COULD HAPPEN

The law firm of Timkins, Mange, and Jaundice had been around for ten years. At first, the tight-knit criminal defense firm tried to market themselves as TMJ, which is the acronym for the disease colloquially called 'Lockjaw'. They thought it'd be clever and memorable enough that everyone would know who they were. They were right, but being attorneys with a rumored disease of the mouth just wasn't what people were looking for in legal representation. Plus two of the partners were already named Mitchell Jaundice and Timothy Mange, so, after their first disastrous marketing campaign, the partners decided they'd better hire some people who aren't named after diseases and, thus, change their image fast. That's when Butler Robinson and a slew of other young defenders were hired. They also made Dorothy Postpartumdepression a partner, not realizing until later their mistake.

    The offices of Timkins, Mange, Jaundice and Postpartumdepression are located on the twenty-fifth floor of a forty-two story skyscraper in midtown Atlanta. It was the epitome of all that a law office should be. There was a mini law library full of Georgia, federal, county, and city ordinances. There were impeccably dressed secretaries, who, while they aren't called secretaries anymore, still manage to do the exact same thing as the "administrative assistants" of the past. There were big windows so that the lawyers can look at all of the little people, pity them, and devise strategies for taking their money. There was music, sort of: hits of the seventies with the words removed so that you can recognize the tune and maybe hum along but not actually get distracted, take off your shirt, funnel a beer and make out with the cute Guatemalan lady who cleans the office.

Butler Robinson was firmly ensconced in the law library. He was researching case law for an upcoming trial wherein Timothy Mange was defending a man who was allegedly selling internet videos of his daughters fornicating with less common household items--the tape of his sixteen year old and the hot water heater is good, but the footage of his eighteen year old, a weed-whacker, the family ferret, and a table saw…priceless. Butler was in the middle of a three day law book and over-the-counter speed binge and needed a break. Call it synchronicity or fate, but Johnny B and Dumpy walked in just as Butler was rubbing his eyes and dreaming about how nice it might be to work in a slaughterhouse, or a jail, or as a fluffer on a porn set, or anywhere but there.

They don't mean to do it, but it happens often anyway. And today was one of those days when Johnny B and Dumpy were wearing matching outfits by accident (granted when half of your pants selections are of the surplus Army camo variety, as are your brother's, then the likelihood of the fashion faux pas goes up dramatically). And when the assembled partners, associates, and assistants of Timkins, Mange, Postpartumdepression and Jaundice saw two large, uncouth, camouflage clad men with four day facial hair on their burly faces and plugs of Beechnut in their mouths enter the office, they were all stunned and tried to look busy enough that they wouldn't be solicited by the men for legal advice, spare change, buttermilk biscuits, or whatever rednecks want. Butler saw them coming through one of the many windows which function as both viewing lenses and confirmations to the associates that only partners should be afforded privacy. Butler knew how futile it'd be to try and hide from the Jones boys. He was too tired to physically jump behind a chair anyway, and just let it happen.

"Uh ma'am, can you tell us where Butler Robinson's at?"

The sexy front desk phone monkey that the firm had hired pointed Johnny B and Dumpy toward the library, where they found Butler's head drooping in and out of that stage of non-alertness where the body is exhausted but the brain is telling you that you have to go on. You've seen it happen to college students and meth addicts alike (and there's some crossover there); the head droops as if toward sleep but then snaps back for another semi-lucid five minutes before it droops again. Whatever, Butler was tired and he was cornered.

"Hey, fellas. It's uh, well, it's a surprise to see you two. What's going on?"

"Not bad. I guess you heard about the lottery."

"Yeah, mom called me a few weeks ago and I saw the footage. Congratulations, if anyone deserves it, it's you; well, that's not true. If anyone deserves it, it's Dee."

Smiling, "Sounds 'bout right."

"Grab some chairs and tell me what I can do for you? Do you need water or a Coke or something?"

"We need a lawyer."

"Oh, what happened? Are y'all in trouble? Already?"

"No. I mean, I don't think so, but we still gonna need a lawyer."

"You know this is a criminal defense firm, right boys? We defend people who're charged with crimes."

"Just like on the TV."

"Yeah, kind of. But it sounds like you need a tax attorney and a CPA, maybe an investment advisor. A lot of them are lawyers too, but they don't have to..."

"No, we want you to be our lawyer and to come with us for this meeting thing today."

"Even though I don't know tax law?"

"Don't matter. We trust you. What do you say?"

"I say yes, but I'm going to have to run it by the partners here, and FYI, I'm not cheap."

"We can afford it now, but drop the legal talk. Like we're gonna know what FYI means."

"Uh, OK. I'll, uh, just go talk to a few people. Y'all stay here. There's water in the pitcher and the fruit's plastic."

The partners were confused but always appreciative of an associate taking initiative and bringing in whales, even whales on a probable monetary crash diet like the Joneses. Although the Joneses didn't yet need a criminal defense attorney, they will. While discussing their pending meeting with Wilkes, Dumpy forgot Butler's admonition and bit into a fake peach.

"Their fruit sucks."

"It's fake, Dump."

"I'm just saying I've had better. You really wanna bring Ethcl's kid to meet with this gangster guy? Butler ain't all that intimidating."

"We don't need a lawyer on steroids, just a briefcase and a tie."

Returning with a smile, Butler brought the paperwork, which, once signed, confirmed his position as the family's official attorney. It was an arrangement which truly benefited both sides, like the rhinoceros and those little birds that eat bugs off their yummy rhino backs.

SOUTHERN ITALIAN

Italian restaurants have a certain feel to them, and the nice ones all feel the same. There's an aura of subdued elegance, of rich foods and rich people, of dim lights and good wine, of good food and bad people. But a lot of that's from TV.

America loves its gangsters: Jesse James wasn't exactly a saint, but people remember him and not the cops who were chasing him. John Dillinger was a fucking madman. Al Capone killed more people than anthrax. Billy the Kid held people up at gunpoint. And we only remember Elliot Ness because he got Capone, and 'lawman' Pat Garrett because he killed Billy the Kid (and Garrett was a former 'bad guy' himself, anyway). Even John Hancock did some smuggling. These are some of our heroes. And not just the obvious outlaws: our tiny little navy during the Revolutionary War was really just a bunch of pirates whom we politely called privateers. Lucky Luciano and Meyer Lansky are reputed to have helped arm Allied troops during WWII. And if you've ever listened to rap music you've got to agree with this simple fact: America loves its outlaws.

And Wilkes was an outlaw.

PH was right. Wilkes was a gangster: not so much in the kick-your-ass-in-an--alley-if-you-don't-pay-us-for-protection kind of way, more of an entrepreneur-who-doesn't-mind-shooting-you kind of way--extreme capitalism, that's the essence of the mob. It's just business cubed.

Wilkes and three of his associates were seated at the back booth, sipping Chianti, talking football, and half-heartedly reviewing some papers when the trio of Dumpy, Johnny B, and their new lawyer, Butler, entered Fellini's. It was three-thirty in the afternoon on a Wednesday, so the place was deserted except for staff and the casually dressy foursome in the back booth.

Wilkes was dressed in a blue blazer, khaki pants, and loafers: more like the attire of every alumnus at a Yale class reunion ever than what you'd expect gangsters to wear, but that was the point. Looking up from the newspaper with that weekend's line, Wilkes recognized Johnny B and Dumpy as they slowly walked into the rear section of Fellini's.

Spotting the crew, Wilkes motioned for them to join his table. As they did, Wilkes' boys left the table, walking slowly toward the kitchen area. Dumpy and Johnny B were calm, although Dumpy was fingering his new ankle-holstered handgun he'd bought to feel more like T.J. Hooker, a hero of his. Employing his legendary lack of subtlety, Johnny B began:

"So I hear you're in the mob?"

Smiling slightly and chuckling, Wilkes answered. "That's just because I'm Italian. You know, all those gangster movies aren't really helping us with our reputations. But, at least creditors are afraid of us. Who's this?"

"Our lawyer."

"Butler Robinson, Mr. Wilkes, nice to meet you."

They shook hands. Butler tried to look confident. Wilkes hadn't thought that the boys would be even this prepared, but he was a man who rolled with the punches, except when he was delivering them.

"OK. Well, the restaurant business has been good to me and I was wondering what you two budding entrepreneurs thought about opening an eatery or two in Comment?"

They thought for a minute. Then they conferred. Then they debated.

"We don't have any place that serves venison?"

"Or squirrel. Man, Butler how many times have you had a hankerin' for some squirrel and then you realize that KFC only serves chicken and then you're all like, damn?"

"Uh, never."

"Well, not me. And J B, remember when we was talking about how there's only like four flavors of milkshake at the Milky Way and you were asking why they didn't have no meat flavored shakes, like pork? Remember? You said you could sell a meal with a built-in desert."

"Uh, guys. I know you know Comment, but I've opened more than my fair share of restaurants and I just don't think anybody is actually looking for meat shakes."

"You may be right, Wilkes. But what about a maple syrup fountain in the middle of town? Think on it. It's got a lot of uses. The kids could play in the syrup when it's hot. And mommas could collect the syrup for cooking. You could bring your waffles. And bees, man the bees would love it."

"You know, that's true, Dump. We don't have a syrup fountain, so that means we probably need one, right?"

"Maybe." Wilkes left to bring them drinks and appetizers.

"OK, OK, you don't like that. What about a library where we charge the people to check out the books and then they could keep them?"

"They have those. They're called book stores, Dumpy."

"Well, we don't need that. What about a water slide?"

"Or a beer slide."

"But the kids can't ride a beer slide."

"OK then, a mouthwash slide. Then you can have fun and your breath will smell good. What you think, Butler?"

"Um, maybe. But, A-you've got an unnatural connection to slides, and B-don't you think the mouthwash will get kind of gross after children roll around in it, kind of defeating the purpose?"

"OK, OK. What about a car wash then? People love carwashes. What about a car wash where you can bring your kids and your pets so they can get clean too. And there could be people there to dry you off and people to play with your pets."

"Or maybe just a car wash for cars?"

Butler was trying to add a dash of sanity to the mix, but clearly this recipe' didn't call for it.

"A little boring, don't you think? Maybe if we put high school girls in bikinis in there, like all those church car washes do."

"We can do better than the churches. The girls could be topless."

"OK, that's definitely illegal, boys. I know I'm just your lawyer, but maybe you should keep on brainstorming."

Wilkes returned with beer and chicken wings which did momentarily shut down the worst brainstorming session since the one in the mid seventies which led to the conversation pit. After the blue cheese ramekins were emptied, the celery left untouched, and the little bones piled high, Johnny B, Dumpy, and Butler cordially said their good-byes. Wilkes agreed to meet them at the Corner in a week to discuss progress and hopefully sign some papers.

Wandering the streets of Atlanta after the meeting, Butler decided that a walk through Centennial Park might be mind-clearing. Centennial Park was constructed as a part of the city's expansion before the 1996 Summer Olympics, celebrating the modern Olympic centennial and not the city's anniversary. It's as picturesque as a downtown park can be, and its running water, a common park technique, somehow always has a calming effect. After procuring two corn dogs and a not dog (veggie-dog) for Butler (while not a vegetarian, Butler Robinson was one of those rare, crazy, traitorously unpatriotic Americans who wants to know what's inside the food he's eating--fucking commie), the three sat on a knee-high red brick wall next to one of the open-air fountains and spoke.

"Oh hey, did y'all get the impression that Wilkes might not be the, uh, legitimate businessman that he says he is?"

"Yeah, PH said he was a gangster, but doesn't look like one. Plus, don't those mob guys make money?"

"Yeah, but for themselves, not for you. You sure you want to keep on talking with him?"

"Let's see what he offers before we dump him."

"You're the bosses."

Johnny B and Dumpy liked the sound of that. It was then that they noticed a female threesome (plus baby) strolling across Centennial Park. The ladies looked a lot like Butler's mom, Ethel, Johnny's wife, Dee, and her daughter Sparkles. The ladies looked like those women mainly because they were...but also because there are a lot of fat women in Georgia. Johnny B's eyes widened as he leapt behind the three-foot brick wall, pulling Dumpy and Butler with him and then flattening them both to the ground where they stayed still and silent until the ladies had passed.

Ethel Robinson had asked Dee to join her for a shopping trip in Atlanta--the big city, the Standing Peachtree, the home of the brave, or at least the Braves, the city formerly known as Marthasville and prior to that, Terminus. Before the Joneses were rich, Dee had accompanied Ethel to Atlanta on numerous 'shopping/getting hair done at ludicrously overpriced salon/pay people to kiss your ass' kind of trips. Dee was Ethel's trusted companion/bag carrier/polydentured servant. But the dynamic had changed, well not completely changed, rather shifted to something new. We all tend to stick in our comfortable little pre-ordained roles even after a life changing event, at least for a while. Since they were still in the transition period, Dee was continuing to carry Ethel's bags for her, but now they split the check.

Like those wacky, sadistic, largely misguided European missionaries with semi- good intentions sent to America to Christianize the Indians or the new manager at Hardee's who comes in and imposes a Japanese work ethic, Ethel was showing Dee how women who don't have to buy used diapers shop. They spend money on clothes that accentuate the positive and eliminate, as much as femininely possible, the negative. Sometimes they mess with Mister In-between, but only if he's on sale. It was all so foreign to Dee: scary, but in a pretty good way.

Ethel had led Dee, Sparkles and Oh-Oh in his new baby papoose through the upscale Atlanta mall known as Phipps Plaza. They'd eaten in the upscale food court (a strange mix of non-oxymoronic, expensive, relatively fast, food). They'd gotten manicures from the Korean women, the acceptable modern outlet for American women who wish they lived in the time of shoe shine boys. Then they went on a tour at the Coca-Cola museum and strolled through Centennial Park.

"Hey, that looks like Johnny B."

"Naw momma, what would daddy be doing in Hotlanta?"

"And isn't that my son, Butler?"

A drunk man dropped a bottle of Mad Dog ten feet away from the women. It shattered, and, as the three ladies' heads were turned to see what had happened, Johnny B took advantage and pulled Dumpy and Butler over the mini-wall.

"Just a drunk."

"Where'd those guys go?"

"Who?"

"The guy who looked like daddy."

"I don't know."

"It's time to introduce you to the world of facials."

"That where they roll you in green mud and smear stuff on your face?"

"Yes, but trust me, it's a good thing."

"OK, but after let's go back to the rich lady mall with all the homos."

CHAPTER TWELVE--ASK A JONES

Wednesdays at Ethel Robinson's house in the Harringtons mean two things: mashed potatoes and gossip. Until her knees gave out and she became physically unable to stand up long enough to properly delump these Irish/South American miracles, Ethel used to mash tubers and make gravy every Wednesday. It was something her mother did, and Ethel, like most children, unconsciously copied many of her mother's rituals. In fact, the Wednesday as Potato day went back eight generations to Mrs. Yolanda S. Vidalia, a gruff but lovable mother of seventeen whose husband was a leading local Whig politician. One hump day, Mrs. Vidalia, although originally from onion stock, declared herself and all of her offspring to be potato people, sending minor shockwaves throughout nowhere, but forever cementing Wednesdays as ceremonial and loaded with carbohydrates for generations. It's like the butterfly flapping its wings in Central Park, only not anything at all like that.

Once Ethel's knees had rendered her incapacitated beyond potato mashing territory, Dee began doing the actual cooking while Ethel sat and occasionally bestowed helpful suggestions/polite orders. Dee also brought a new wrinkle to the ritual. She added gossip. Before Hannah was fired, the mother daughter dust-busting combo came to Ethel's on Tuesdays and Fridays, but Dee, separate from and unbeknownst to her mother, began coming here almost every day. And this was Wednesday.

"No, for real Ethel. The mayor even called and everything."

"This is actually going to happen?"

"Maybe. They were def'nitly gonna have it, but after our news footage made it to the Internet, the mayor called back and kind of cancelled on us, maybe."

"That little turd."

"Oooh Ethel, it's OK. I can do without the fussin' over us. Come on, a city block party, that's too much for one family."

"I suppose. But you're still going to be on that radio call-in show in Atlanta?"

"Day after tomorrow. I'm so nervous. Could you call in, Miss Ethel, and ask a really easy question?"

"I'd love to, Dee, if I can get through. Anything specific you'd like me to ask?"

"Uh, I don't know. Ask about Oh-Oh, or how I feel, or just something easy."

"Sounds like fun."

"Maybe for you. I'm worse nervous than when Uncle P was in the ICU for trying to eat all them tree frogs, the druggy ones."

"Those exotic pet stores, they'll be the death of all of us."

"You said it, Miss Ethel."

Meanwhile, at the Corner, Johnny B and Dumpy's unofficial headquarters, Billy, the angry, Napoleonic employee, was cussing under his breath about having to mop up peanut shells, cigarette butts, and any spare toupees lost in last night's drunken haze.

"Stupid fake hair drunk bastards."

"What's that, Billy?"

"Nothing, sir."

The brothers were attempting to look at a spreadsheet and hopefully become knowledgeable enough to be able to at least fake their way through the upcoming discussion that will ensue once Butler finishes using the restroom.

"Can't make heads or tails of it, Dump."

"It's easy, brother. I think. This column up here looks like what we spend on like beer and peanuts and all. And this, I hope, is the money we take in. Yeah, yeah, I think I get it. As long as this one's bigger than this one, we're making money."

"Are we?"
"Are we what?"
"Making money?"
"Hell if I know."

Emerging from the restroom hallway and wiping his hands on the back of his snazzy chinos, Butler answers the overheard question.

"Yes, you two are making money...not much, not yet, but honestly, you two've made more in the last month than PH did for all of the last fiscal year."

"Shhh, he's right over there."

"I can hear you. Y'all ain't sneaky. But don't worry. I don't care that you're better at running this place than me. I'm set with the cash from the sale, so I don't care."

"Thanks, PH."

"Yeah, appreciate it, hoss. So, Butler, what's our next move?"

"Well, what do you want it to be? Remember, I work for you, not the other way around."

"Yeah, me and Dump's been discussing this. You know, stuff that we need here in Comment. And we only got the one barbeque place, and ya know people like ribs around here. And we don't have any used car lots."

"And no mud wrasslin at all."

"That's true, Dump. Nowhere a man can go and watch two young girls get close to nekked and fight each other."

"Does Comment need that?"

"Hell, **I** need that. You think Elaine lets me buy Penthouse?"

"I suppose not."

"Oh hey, Butler, that Wilkes guy called while you were in the crapper. He moved the time up to, what'd he say Dump, like twenty minutes."

"So, he's on his way right now?"

"Yep. You want a snack before he gets here?"

"Sure."

"Billy, go back to the kitchen and cook us up some buffalo wings."

Under his breath, "I'll cook your buffalo wings."

Once Billy was in the kitchen, it struck the owners that their dwarflike employee might need a better outlet for his pain than random mutterings to no one. The next day they bought him a set of oriental stress balls which lasted exactly six minutes until he threw them at a stray dog who vaguely resembled Dumpy, only relieving Billy's stress for a brief moment, but calming the dog down quite a bit.

Once the wings were cooked and eaten and the question of why the average animal observer can't see the buffalo's tiny wings until after they're cooked was answered to everyone's satisfaction, a sharp dressed man walked into the Corner. Every girl there would've gone crazy, but, of course, there were no females present. So everyone stayed sane.

Wilkes had brought three of his boys, all of whom had arms the size of oscillating fans, and necks which looked thick enough to support Easter Island heads. One of them wore a pre-game NBA style jumpsuit; the other two were dressed more golf casual with Polo shirts and visors. The three "associates" all sat at a different table.

"Hey, Wilkes. We don't even get introductions?"

"What, to those guys? Their names don't matter."

The three men would've protested, but they knew he was right.

"OK, well, have a seat. You wanna drink?"

"Uh, no, I'm fine. Hi, lawyer."

"I don't really like to go by lawy'..."

"I've been thinking about some investment possibilities for you two."

"And?"

"Back at my office, I tried to brainstorm and think about what you guys would be into. It helps if you're excited about your investments. I was tossing around the idea of opening a brewery myself a few years back, what about instead, you two guys open one? I'll be your silent partner and take care of the boring money stuff, and you two can concentrate on the product. You guys like beer, don't you?"

"Does a dog shit in the woods?"

"It's a bear, Dump."

"What's a bear?"

"Who shits in the woods. The bear shits in the woods."

"There ain't room for a dog and a bear? Woods is big."

"There is, just, you know, don't worry about it. Mr. Wilkes, what else have you got?"

"It's just Wilkes. I bought out the franchise contract of the Dollar Shop down the street. I could let you two run it and we could split the profits."

"Maybe. Could be fun. We'll think about it."

"Don't take too long. This is a good opportunity." With that, Wilkes nodded and walked out, his three bodyguards in tow.

"He looked mad."

"Yeah, I know."

Ph couldn't resist throwing his two cents in with an I-told-you-so. Everybody does, or at least wants to.

"I like that brewery idea…Dumpy B's beer?"

"Or Johnny and Dump's Special brew."

"Johnny's Special Dump."

And the two of them continued to "brain"storm for twenty minutes, coming up with some of the least appetizing names for food products since the invention of the breakfast burrito (two words which, in a perfect world, would repel each other like similarly charged magnets, but clearly we don't live in a perfect world).

After excusing himself, Butler called Wilkes via cell phone to say that the two would definitely buy the Dollar Shop from Wilkes, but other than that, they would not be needing his services. Wilkes seemed less than thrilled.

ANSWERS

"Hey everybody. It's Chris White coming back at you here at WDHS, the Troll!!

Last week's call-in show went really well. Thanks again to everybody who called about our age of consent debate. That one was a rager, but I think we can all agree that there needs to at least be grass on the field. Today, we've got local celebrity family and the newest Comment millionaires, the Jones family. I'm sure we all remember the news footage of them receiving the big check. In the studio today we've got Johnny B Jones, his lovely wife, Diedre, Johnny's brother, Dumpy. Is that right, Dumpy? Yeah. OK, we've got those three and Jones family female heartthrob, Charity. Charity, I understand your social life has picked up quite a bit since that day at the Piggly-Wiggly?"

Charity---"Um, yeah, Chris. I got all kinds of dates, maybe too many. But if any boy bands are listening, call me anyway. I like dancin'; I watched the Mickey Mouse Club, and I love frosted hair."

Chris--"OK. While we're waiting for callers, and don't worry, my call screener, Corby, will tell us when we've got somebody, let me ask you a question, Johnny. What's it like, my man?"

Johnny--"What, bein' rich? It's cool. You can buy a lot more stuff. Oh and now I know that poor people will do whatever you want if you pay them. Man, it's great, I got the pizza delivery boy to deliver nekked, just 'cause I promised him fifty bucks. Man, ain't nothing funnier than a nekked pizza boy when you're drunk. Now I only use Evian bottles for spitters. Oh and I got this homeless guy to have sex with a tree."

Chris---"OK, OK. That's interesting, disgusting and most likely violates some health codes, but Mr. Jones raises a good point. People will do anything for money. If you've ever done anything weird for money, call in and share your story, unless it's prostitution. That's not all that weird. I was thinking that we..."

Dee--"Can I say hey to someone?"

Chris---"Sure."

Dee--"Hey, Jesus."

Chris---"Um, alright. Corby, have we got our first caller? OK, here goes. Hey caller, you're on The Troll. What's your name?"

Caller #1--"Name's Reginald. And my question is for Johnny B. So, if a man makes a heap of money, does he need to pay back people he owes?"

Johnny--"Reggie, you stupid BLEEP, I done paid yer worthless BLEEP last week. Don't give me any of this interest bullBLEEP. You were paid, and you know it ain't nothing to me to whoop a man's BLEEP."

Chris---"OK, thank God for the cough button. And Corby, you might want to reread the job description of Call Screener or see if Burger King is hiring fry cooks. Next up we have Delinda with a question for Mrs. Jones. Go ahead Delinda, you're on the Troll."

Caller #2---"Yeah, I just wanted to ask Diedre where she got them jean shorts she was wearing on the TV. I can't find any in my size and her butt looks about my size."

Dee---"How big is your butt?"

Caller #2—"Bout a handful for each cheek."

Dee—"Mine too!"

Caller #2—"The shorts?"

Dee--"Where you think? I got 'em at the Mart, but I think it's time to start shopping at Target like all them rich folks."

Chris---"Thank you, caller. It looks like Commenteers are the callers today. Is that what you call yourselves, people from Comment? Commenteers? Commenters? Commentarians? Call and enlighten us."

Dumpy--"I think we're called Comers. Ain't that right, Charity?"

Charity was too busy laughing at her uncle's inadvertent sexual reference to answer.

Dee--"I think it's Commenteers."

Chris---"I think we need a new caller...fast. We've got one? All right. Listeners, we've got Deshon on the line from Perry, Georgia. Go for it Deshon, you're on the Troll."

Deshon---"Hey Chris. You've got a cool radio voice. My question is for Johnny. I saw you on TV and I'm black. Anyway, I wanted to give you a chance to apologize for the racist stuff you said on TV...shut up, Joey, I'm trying to do something good...Chris, my boyfriend is telling me to call them white devils, but I don't think anyone says that anymore, do they?"

Chris---"Um, I'm a little confused. OK, we all saw the footage, and I believe Deshon here is being <u>very</u> generous and giving y'all a chance to apologize to the black community."

Johnny---"Oh yeah. Hey, we're sorry. I ain't got no problem with nobody of any color, black, white, Mexican. I mean, I want to invite all coloreds to come to a party we're having downtown next Saturday. I'll even put up a big banner that says, "Coloreds Welcome.""

Chris—"Yeah, Johnny I wouldn't do that if I were you."

Johnny—"Yeah, well, you ain't me."

Charity—"I bet he wishes he wuz you, daddy."

Chris—"Um, sure. Corby, who's up next?"

Corby---"OK, we've got Mickey Collin on line three."

Chris---"OK, Mickey, go ahead, you're on the Troll....Mickey, are you there?"

Mickey—"Yeah, aaiight. Sorry, I dropped the phone. Somebody bumped me in line at the free clinic. Name's Mickey Collin. My question is for Charity? Those things real, baby?"

Johnny—"You seriously asking that in front of her daddy?"

Mickey—"Well good luck figurin' out who I am over the phone."

Dee---"You said your full name, idiot."

Mickey—"Oh crap. Maybe it was a fake name."

Johnny---"You stupid BLEEP. I BLEEPing know you. You work down at Donald's Dried Fruits. Better run, boy."

Charity—"But yeah, they're real."

Johnny—"Don't be saying that on the radio. Wait Charity, he was talking about your girly parts right?"

Charity—"Naw daddy, he was talking about my boobies."

Chris—"OK, moving on. I know a lot of our listeners would like to know what the first thing y'all did after getting the big check."

Dee—"We went shopping. What else?"

Dumpy---"Not me, hoss. I called all my old teachers and parole officers to tell them to kiss my BLEEPING BLEEP. Wait, I can't say BLEEP on the BLEEPing radio? What kind of BLEEP is that?"

Chris---"My finger is now cramping from having to delete all of your more colorful language. So, we're going to wrap it up before the FCC comes in here with billy clubs. How about one more caller, Corby?"

Corby—"We've got Conrad on the line from Crandall."

Chris—"Go ahead, Conrad. You're on the Troll."

Conrad---"Uh yeah. Hey Chris, you're cool, man. Hey Dumpy, you still got my lug wrench man?"

Dumpy—"Um, naw. I pawned it to buy some jewelry for my girl, Elaine. Hey Lanie, love you always, cute stuff. But hey, Conrad, come by the Corner and I'll get you a new one. Hell, I'll buy Craftsman, the good stuff."

Conrad—"Cool. You're alright, Dump. Hey, what ever happened with that purple rash…"

Chris---"Once again, we're going to have to cut our program short. But it was, without a doubt, one of the more interesting programs we've had here on the Troll. Don't forget, everyone, next week we've got author Perry Duncan from Alba and the week after we've got a traveling band from Baltimore called the Sketch Artists. And people, remember that you cannot, I repeat, cannot use cuss words on the air."

Dumpy---"But you can BLEEPing try."

Chris---"Later, Georgia."

CHAPTER THIRTEEN—THE EVERCHANGING FACE OF REALITY

"What is this crap? Why does everybody just trash all our stuff since we got rich?"

It was a good question. Upon returning from the radio call-in show, the Joneses discovered that someone had trashed the Corner.

"First your crazy ass mom at our new house and now this shit. Dee, honey, is this your momma again?"

"I don't think so. She wouldn't set foot in a bar, even to send you a message."

"That's true. She once told me that all the drinkers are gonna wind up in the same escalator in hell, and we all have to massage the shoulders of all the people we've vomited on."

"Well, you've puked on me twice…get to rubbin'. Ya know, your mom's idea of religion is a little weird, you know."

"She's been to a lot of different churches in her life. I think she picks out the parts she likes from each one."

"No dumber than anybody else."

The Joneses, of course, called the Comment police department. The CPD sent out the same two officers as they had when Hannah had trashed Jones manor. Granted, the CPD only had two officers with all of their fingers and a working excretory system, but the Joneses didn't know that. The other officer tandem, consisting of the guy with a thumb and five other fingers scattered conservatively up and down his only remaining arm and his incontinent partner with the full-body adult diaper suit, doesn't get sent out on many non-'See the World's Smallest Horse' related calls.

Officer Eckstein and Sergeant Peterson were more confident that they would emerge alive from this encounter with the Joneses than they had been on their previous visit. It didn't hurt that Dee was offering jars of homemade jam, two lambs, and her eldest daughter to Officer Eckstein as penance. The officer, while he, as anyone would, enjoyed being worshipped, felt that Internal Affairs might have a problem with his having accepted human chattel as a reward for simply doing his job. He did take the lambs though.

"Mr. Jones, I don't know what to say. You know what they say about all that lottery curse stuff. I thought that was all urban legend like the alligators in the sewer or midgets being real, but either it's true or you've just got some amazing bad luck."

"Maybe both, officer. You want a drink, Coke, tall boy or something?"

"We're fine. On duty. We'll file a report, but it'd take a few more resources than we have to do any actual investigation."

"What do you mean?"

"I mean, we don't exactly have a Crime Scene team, like they do on television. We've got some stuff that looks like it might be fingerprint powder back at the station, but you know that could be from the time we arrested that clown. Peterson, do you know?"

"I'll call the chief."

After ascertaining that the Comment police force did in fact have no fingerprint powder, but an oddly impressive supply of clown makeup, the officers filed their report and promised that they'd do more, but left the details kind of vague. Johnny B knew the deal. The Comment police force meant well, it really did, but they just weren't a force. Two relatively healthy cops, an aging chief, a cripple and an incontinent—it's not exactly the Justice League of America. Besides, Comment's always been more of a vigilante justice kind of town. It is near the sight of America's first non-El Dorado gold rush. And vigilante justice was one of those tings that just went along with gold rush boom towns, like cultural tension, violence and syphilis. Therefore, Johnny B and Dumpy correctly guessed that they were probably going to have to deal with this thing themselves.

MOTHER AND CHILD REUNION
Dee, Sparkles, and the baby were at the Harringtons talking to Ethel Robinson about the strange events of the past week. They were also holding a try out for Ethel's new maid. Although Dee hadn't wanted to give up cleaning Ethel's house, Ethel had cooked up another recipe for cleanliness. Dee would stay on as an unpaid janitorial consultant—she would be able to boss the new maid around and still generally determine the outcome of the cleaning ritual. Ethel, Sparkles and Dee had put a classified ad in the paper for a Maid Try Out a few weeks ago:

Do you clean houses for a living?

Are you good under pressure?

Come to the Robinson Maidtastic Try Out this Saturday afternoon.

BYO mop

There were five possible replacements for Dee present that afternoon. Dee and Sparkles had set up four feats of cleanliness for the clamoring contestants. First off, the maids-in-waiting had to search through a vat of mashed potatoes for one of Oh-Oh's favorite toys (Ethel had a lot of left over mashed potatoes)—they're judged on time. Second, the contestants had to hurl the baby onto a mattress for distance (as preparation for when the baby is approaching dangerous situations like a hungry she-bear or a box of lives wolves and used hypodermic needles). Third, the possibles had to sweep and vacuum their way through a pre-arranged obstacle course of furniture, piles of dirty clothes, and a life-sized cardboard cut-out of Winston Churchill (Ethel's mother had had a rather disturbing crush on him during the war). Again, they're judged on time. And finally, the five hopefuls had to write a standard five paragraph essay about what they did last summer (Ethel was a retired school teacher---it's just habit). Whichever essay had the fewest grammatical mistakes was to win.

Of course, three of the hopefuls left when they found out there was grammar involved. But those two ladies who stayed went through the whole gamut. Stacy Rigger and Jo Anne Butterfield both performed admirably. The judging committee was torn and so they compromised on Stacy coming on Wednesdays and Jo Anne on Fridays. Dee would come both days and politely order them around.

"That was an ordeal, now, wasn't it, Miss Ethel?"

"Indeed, Dee. Hey, now that we're done, how would you feel about bailing your mother out of jail?"

"OK, I guess it's about time we got her out. Nestor, her new husband, won't even go near the jail. I think he's illegal or has some warrants out for him, or something."

"Well, we could go."

"OK, just let me send the new maids home, Miss Ethel, and we'll go."

"Nervous?"

"About seeing my mom? Worse than labor."

EVERYTHING UNDER THE SUN FOR ONLY A DOLLAR

Johnny B, Dumpy, Elaine and Butler Robinson threw open the doors of their latest purchase: The Dollar Shop. First off, these are great stores. And since politicians and money men have been trying their damndest lately to kill the middle class, this is where a large percentage of America shops. Come on, where else can you get a side of beef, a sixty-four pack of crayons with optional sharpener, cold medication, spark plugs, and a few scratch offs for $6.75?

The family had discussed the possibilities for the store and Elaine, after once again threatening to leave Dumpy for the Pakistani man who runs the hardware store, was granted dominion over The Dollar Shop. Elaine had a plan, more of a rough sketch actually. She was going to sell all of the standard dollar merchandise, but add a hair and nail salon, a delivery service, and offer a five thousand dollar reward for the capture of Miss Lola Jane Copeland, dead or alive.

Butler had arranged a moving crew to come in and reshuffle the store, adding whatever Elaine wants and basically Jonesifying the entire place. It's a week long job.

MOB MENTALITY

Six swarthy men sat in ornate mahogany chairs in a secluded back room of an upscale Italian restaurant in downtown Atlanta. They meet here once a week to discuss the progress of their criminal empire. If you get right down to it, their meetings really aren't all that different from most corporate board of director's quarterly meetings. Wilkes was like the CFO of this particular "family". He wasn't the head guy, but he was damn close. Four of the "directors" present represent the work force—the middle management, if you will. Today, the CEO himself was present, and he was curious. Mr. D hadn't planned on being a mob boss, at least not in the way that gangster movies would have you believe. He had an MBA from Colgate; he wore classy, but not over-the-top gaudy suits; he had freckles; he ate more Mexican food than Italian; he didn't even have a mistress. Still, he was the boss, the man behind the man behind the man. And today, the man behind the man was worried about the third quarter's profits.

"Wilkes, what about the thing with the big guy?"

"Which big guy?"

"The big guy with the ice cream."

"Good. He settled up with only minor convincing."

"And the thing with the construction?"

"On schedule."

"The thing with the cell phones?"

"A little slower than we thought, but we're in negotiations."

"OK, what about that thing you were so excited about, the thing with the two fat guys out in the sticks?"

"Being dealt with. I should have an update for you next week."

"Make sure that you do, Wilkes. Nobody's irreplaceable, not even you."

"Yes sir. Gino, get the boss some appetizers."

"No don't, Gino. I had a chalupa on the way over here."

Once MR. D had left to survey other aspects of his nation-wide semi-legitimate empire, Wilkes took the boys out back. Next to the glow of the streetlight reflected off the spilled motor oil in the alley, Wilkes laid out his plan for the Joneses.

"OK boys. We trashed that sneaky little lawyer fuck's office and we trashed the bar where the fat guys work. Now we wait a day and let them think about what could be next. We've got to give them time to get scared. Tomorrow we meet here and you take care of the lawyer and then go down there to that redneck town around dusk and either they pay or well, you guys do your thing. Got it?"

"Yeah, boss."

"Sure thing, boss."

"OK, well be here at three and Benny, don't wear the short sleeve white button down, you look like your there to fix their computer and not shit down their necks."

"OK, boss. What about jean shorts?"

"Jean shorts? You think cut offs are intimidating? Dear God! Did Capone have to deal with this crap? Did Bugsy Seagal? When my mother said, 'Wilkes, everybody loves a dentist', did I listen?"

The henchmen left Wilkes alone in the alley to mutter about paths not taken. They had to hurry. It was their bowling league night.

FAMILY—WHAT A CONCEPT

The Comment Correctional Facility is, as you might imagine, a small operation. Housed in a former drive-through coffee shop, the cells are closer to Torquemada levels of decency than any facility outside of medieval Spain or modern day Texas. Hannah's the only woman currently in jail. Bertrand Ignacious Featherman, aka Bif, was the lone occupant of the men's side, but he'd been there so long that none of the cops could remember why he was arrested in the first place, although they vaguely remembered something having to do with power tools. They knew that he was cheap to feed and hadn't touched his meals for months. Technically, that was because he was dead, but it would be a while before anyone noticed.

Officer Dan White was the incontinent member of the Comment Police Lack of Force. It's not easy being an adult with excretory problems, but it's a living hell when you're twelve years old. Dan had never had a working poopie system, and some would say that the merciless teasing he received daily while growing up actually made his line of work inevitable. In other words, if everybody calls you Poopypants all your life, you're going to need a license to kill. And since MI-6 wasn't hiring, he became a cop. Nobody calls Dan 'Poopypants' anymore, but some of his colleagues do call him Officer Poopypants. It's progress.

Three women and a baby drove up to the bail window in a brand new black Camaro with an orange racing stripe. Officer White, briefly laying aside his 'Guns & Ammo & Catheters' magazine, leaned his head out the window.

"Hey, ladies. What can I do for you today?"

"My momma's in there…Hannah Redmond Mathis Biggins Reed Rodriguez."

"That'll be 300 dollars."

Dee paid the man and the ladies waited as Officer White let Hannah out of her shackles, removed the ball gag, and led her out to the idling Camaro in the light-brown gravel parking/bailing lot. Hannah crawled in the back seat wearing an expression that Dee had never seen on her mother's face—it was the expression of nothing, hopelessness, the kind of look you see on the people's faces being let out of Chinese internment camps, the same look on the faces of people who have just received Electroshock Therapy, or the way really dumb kids looks all the time. Dee was nervous. She'd always been a little nervous around her mother, but this whole role reversal, bailing mom out of jail, life comes full circle thing was messing with Dee's sense of what the world is and where she was located in it. Still, being an optimist at heart, Diedre Jones was not going to let this conciliatory opportunity slip through her calloused fingers.

"Momma, how was it?"

Hannah grunted and they took that for an "it was jail, how do you think it was?" which is what Hannah had meant.

For the time it took Sparkles to drive from the jail to Woodland Springs, Dee tried to think of something that would begin to mend the tattered fence that existed between Hannah and her daughter. Halfway there, Dee realized the best thing that she could do and silently did it. She handed a sleeping Oh-Oh to Hannah to hold. Hannah smiled at her daughter and began to hum a hymn to her great grandson as she gently rocked him in her arms. It was the most beautiful moment those two had shared together in years and it made Ethel and Dee both weep tears of joy. Those are the best cries.

BIENVENIDOS

Nestor had no way of knowing how long Hannah would be in jail. So, as each day passed, Nestor began to incrementally change his dwelling into something more familiar, something that he knew. It seemed more like home to him now. To Hannah it seemed like a Honduran shanty town. Basically, Nestor had Mexicanized the place. If you're one of those knee-jerk PC liberals who won't admit that there are cultural differences, well then you're an idiot, but even you know exactly what I'm talking about when I say Nestor had Mexicanized Hannah's trailer in Woodland Springs, even if you won't admit it out loud for fear of offending someone who technically only exists in your head.

How had Nestor even found that many chickens in two weeks? Why did he drag the stove outside? Why are there now dead, skinned animal carcasses hanging on a line off of her tool shed? Where did this other family come from, and why does Nestor look so comfortable with them?

Nestor, believing his new wife to be lost to him for ever, had sent for his old wife and seven kids. They'd made the arduous journey from Southern Mexico to the Southern United States. Don't let the conservative pundits tell you that border crossings are easy; they're the exact opposite of that. They're the Old West. They're adventure books where someone usually dies. They involve hiding from authority figures, bribery, extreme discomfort, and a lot of prayer…and that's just if you're lucky enough to make it to your destination. Nestor's wife and seven kids had made it, barely, but they had.

Seeing Hannah calmly climb out of Dee's car, Nestor had a slight moment of panic. But, human beings are nothing if not adaptable. Nestor figured that there had to be a way for him to have his cake and eat it too. He had a plan. He would do nothing.

Although normally a reactive hurricane, some time in the jail calmed even this obsessive mountain woman. Hannah hugged Nestor and silently walked inside her trailer, lay down and took a well deserved nap.

Although living arrangements would have to be worked out later, they were. Although Nestor would never tell Hannah that this other woman was his wife and not his sister as Hannah just assumed after the first time she caught him having sex with her and he explained through gesture that that was common practice in Mexico, even that wouldn't break up a marriage which was based on too solid a foundation of fuzzy lies and loving self-delusion to be destroyed by something as simple as polygamy.

IT'S KIND OF FUNNY FOR A SPLIT SECOND
The human mind is a strange, misunderstood and wildly interesting place. For example: When Butler Robinson rang his mother's doorbell, and she saw his badly bruised face, cut cheek and black eye, she laughed for a split second while the reality was setting in. Then she got scared and she-bear motherly, nursing his wounds with ointment and feeding him large amounts of food (the fall back son-raising mothering technique). Then she asked him what had happened.

"Just a work thing, mom, don't worry about it."

"You're a lawyer, Butler, not a prize fighter."

"I wasn't even going to come home, but I knew what you'd do if your heard about this through the Comment grapevine."

"So who did it?"

"Just some business associates…kind of."

"You were physically assaulted at your office?"

"Truthfully, yeah. Three huge guys just walked in and beat the snot out of me and then walked out. Nobody did anything and now the partners are probably thinking of firing me. I swear it was like something out of a bad novel, mother."

"Oh come on, that sounds like a pretty good novel. Anyway, sit down and let me give you some vegetable soup."

"Yeah, that usually mends broken bones." While his mother was failing to pick up on his sarcasm, Butler continued to talk as Ethel carefully bandaged her eldest son. Patching up your sons' injuries—it's like riding a bike or using chopsticks--once you know how to do it, you don't forget. "I came here to meet with your Joneses, mother."

"Why? Do you need personal hygiene advice?"

"Funny. Actually, they smell good nowadays…well maybe good's too strong a word, but better. Anyway, I'm their lawyer."

"Yeah, Dee told me something about that. Will wonders never cease?"

Johnny B, Dumpy and their angry miniature employee, Billy, were slowly cleaning the mess that Wilkes' crew had made of The Corner. Wanting to send a message but not destroy the means by which he would get paid, Wilkes had directed his boys to trash some furniture and break some bottles, but to basically leave the place in tact. According to Wilkes' mob hit spread sheet (standard feature on the new Microsoft Windows Mafia Operating System), this tactic is successful eighty-five point two percent of the time. Usually it scares the people into head-shaking acquiescent submission and they pay up.

It did not have the desired effect on the Jones boys.

CHAPTER FOURTEEN—LOOSE ENDS

There was a palpable sense of fun in the air. It's not like the unfocused sense of euphoria that you see on kids' faces in line at Disneyworld. It's not like that obvious sense of 'the world is right' joy you see on a bride's beaming face. It's more like when the traveling medicine show rolls through town, or when a B list celebrity is going to cut the ribbon at the brand new mini-mall. The Commenteers were excited. And why shouldn't they be? It's a city wide block party. After seeing the Piggly Wiggly footage, the mayor had tried to back out, but people love a party.

Five blocks of Main Street had been cordoned off with police tape. It was, wisely, and much to Dumpy's chagrin, officially an alcohol-free festivity. Granted, judging from the many, many brown paper bags circulating in the crowd, that was more of a suggestion than a regulation.

The first word on the "Coloreds Welcome" banner was scratched off and it now read: "Everybody Welcome, not just Coloreds". They mean well…

People who hadn't changed their routine since the last tornado were out in force. A group of carnies who had been hiding from the GBI in a cave just outside of town had donned their fake ZZ Top beards and black rimmed glasses and fake nose combos and were operating a few of the low rent rides typical of the mobile parade of sadness that is the traveling modern American carnival. There was the ride where you sit in a spinning cup and move around in an up and down circle. There was the one that's a big slide and you sit on a scratchy burlap sack and explore the wonders of gravity while cascading down a five foot high "Super Slide". And there's the one where you stand with your back up against the semi-padded wall and go around in a really fast circle trying to defeat the forces of nature by moving in mid spin. That's the ride that the GA carnie union, Not My Job Local 412, has tried for years to make illegal so that they won't have to clean the massive amounts of congealed saliva on the cushy walls.

There were also candy stands: cotton candy, candied apples, peanut brittle, caramelized peaches, pixie stick surprise, funnel cakes, and homemade fudge. There were hot dog stands, venison burger stands, reconstituted chicken bits stands, possum patties stands, corn dog stands, and a giant vat of Orlando's mashed potatoes where children could frolic and eat their fill (BYO gravy).

Since the theme of the block party was Let's Celebrate The Joneses and their good fortune, there were also Jones themed events at the Comment Block Party. Charity's corner consisted of a kissing booth where she not only had the power of veto, but they paid her to get kissed. She also had set up various feats of strength in a kind of animalistic cave girl search for the ideal mate gauntlet, the centerpiece of which is one of those hit the hammer on the round metal thing which sends the flashing light up the ladder of manliness: Church Choirmaster, Homo, wus, eunuch, junior high wrestler, real man, strong man, and 'Dear God, Don't Hurt Me' were the categories. She also had an arm wrasslin' table, a shirtless Greco-Roman rink, and a semi-circle of hopeful suitors paying her false compliments and begging for scraps at her lascivious table.

Although it hadn't been planned, Dee found herself in the center of an admiring circle of mainly young married women who were looking for the latest gossip, and stretching the definition of flattery to new and exciting levels. Women, who before would have barely tolerated her cleaning their houses, were now asking for Dee's down home advice. She loved every minute of their obvious jealousy. This was one of the happiest moments of her life.

Uncle P even got into the act, albeit by accident. After having smoked two pinecones and drunk a quart of motor oil, Peter had passed out and become the prop for the always popular children's game: 'Pin The Tail on The Junkie'. He might've been surprised when he woke up to find thirty straight pins and blue ribbons in and on him, but he just figured that he'd won yet another beauty contest. Plus, he'd woken up in stranger situations before—this one not even comparing to the time when he woke up in a Donald Duck outfit at the local landfill with his head in a pile of used Ukrainian oatmeal. At least this time won't require any lye or an atlas.

Johnny B and Dumpy were the rock stars of the party, no doubt about it. They were signing body parts (when Dee and Elaine weren't looking), drinking discretely from Pretty Good Market supplied brown paper bags, laughing with everyone, telling stories, and generally having the time of their lives. They were both nursing their beers and drinking slower than they ever had before outside of Easter church service. Hiding flasks in hollowed out Bibles and stashing them liberally through the pews during Lent had sounded like a good plan, but the Lord just doesn't appreciate vomit in His houses of worship. No matter what their degree of sobriety, the boys were enjoying their day.

Sparkles was keeping an eye on Oh-Oh as he was voraciously gobbling down his third funnel cake. She was talking to Ethel and Butler at one of the many picnic tables in front of the Dairy Queen.

The one thing that the Joneses never expected at their party was the arrival of a contrite Hannah. But it happened. Two hours into the festivities, Hannah, Nestor, and Nestor's other wife strolled in. Nestor and his other wife said their holas and left to discover the joys of venison burgers while a surprisingly calm Hannah sat down next to Dee.

"Um, Dee, honey, I just wanted to say…that I um…"

Hannah trailed off as the tears came pouring out volcano style from her dewy, blood-shot eyes. This was as good an apology as if she'd actually used words. And it was enough to make Dee, who'd been anxious to reconcile with her mother, join in the cry. This made Ethel cry, which made Sparkles cry. Butler excused himself and went to bawl in a Port-O-Potty. Oh-Oh finished his third funnel cake and started in on the placemats.

No words were needed for this estranged mother/daughter team to get back to actually being mother and daughter. Apologies aren't about words anyway, not really. Hannah and Dee both would have to settle into their new roles and cast aside a lot of the excess baggage of their old ones. Hannah would have to learn to think before she spoke (which she never did, but did start immediately apologizing after a particularly venomous outburst—beating the previous pattern). Dee would have to learn to put her foot down, to confront her mother in the moment and not to let the anger and resentment build and build until she's in nervous breakdown territory. And she did. There's a Paul Simon song about a mother and child reunion and it's a really beautiful song. It doesn't have much to do with this story, but I like Paul Simon and you're not writing the book, so you're going to hear about it.

After only a few minutes of nonverbal apologies, Hannah was once again holding her grandson in her lap, bouncing him on her knee and stopping him from eating her press-on nails emblazoned with the faces of the Gatlin Brothers. Dee was laughing as she related the story of Hannah's crazy rampage through Jones manor. Ethel was enjoying the show and the cops had used the Jaws of Life to remove Butler from the Port-O-Potty in which he'd been trapped, sobbing and silently cursing everyone.

Johnny B's "Guess How Many Animals I've Strangled With My Bear Hands This Month" contest was also a success. When Raymond Jenkins guessed fifteen the crowd went wild. He received a $500 dollar gift certificate from Madame Wong's One Trip Only Chinese Buffet and a congratulatory hug/photo op from the mayor.

It was a good day for Comment, Georgia. It was going to be a wild night.

OLD SCHOOL THROW DOWN

Leaving their party, the Jones family had retired to the site of their newest entrepreneurial venture (formerly known as the Dollar Shop and fixing to be renamed Elaine's Cheap and Easy—it would be a while before Elaine realized the double entendre). Dragging their lawyer, the eternally nervous Butler Robinson, with them, the Joneses were standing just inside the front entrance, plotting the design of Elaine's Cheap and Easy. Uncle P had removed most of his ribbons and was searching for the whipped cream aisle. Oh-Oh had discovered that tin foil was edible if you have the will power. Dee was relaxing in a pink, folding lawn chair on aisle ten, reminiscing about a day well lived. Butler had brought the legal documents for the Joneses to sign in order that Elaine's Cheap and Easy can become true on multiple levels. Charity was text messaging Brad, the semi-retarded, weight lifting physical therapist with the six pack abs and the seven word vocabulary who'd won her arm wrasslin' tournament and her heart.

That's when the first bullets ripped through the glass doors and landed in the potato chip section. As Cheetos and Funyons flew haphazardly around the store, the Joneses collectively hit the deck. Another hail of ammunition whizzed above the heads of the Jones family and their lawyer, who was still not quite used to the random violence that accompanied representing the Joneses. On the ground, Dee hugged her daughter who hugged her daughter. Dumpy belly crawled to the window and peered over the edge.

"It's Wilkes and his mob boys. JB, you armed?"

"Left it in the truck. Everybody all right?...OK, good. Butler, help Dumpy push stuff up front. We need to block the doors. Dee, get the women to the freezer in the back. Mike, you there? Mike?"

"I'm here."

"You know, Mike, I think that's the first time I've ever heard you talk."

"Now's not the time, Butler."

"Mike, we've got a sawed-off behind the counter. See if you can get it out without standing up."

Another five shots rang out as Dee led the crawling caravan of concerned Southern women toward the freezer section and its promise of possible protection…and ice cream sandwiches. The family unity was in full effect when Charity's spaghetti strap got caught on a vacuum cleaner extension, and Dee had to double back to help her daughter. Hannah, newly reunited with the family, was helping a bawling Sparkles along. If it weren't for the threat of imminent death, this might've been a beautiful family moment.

Wilkes and his three henchmen were standing in a semi-circle on the asphalt blacktop in front of the former Dollar Shop, guns trained on the door. Wilkes knew that he had the family trapped. He'd briefly owned this very property and knew that there was no service entrance. He knew from experience that a torrent of bullets can be an effective negotiating technique. He knew that he could scare almost anyone.

He knew that if he didn't get the boys to sign over a sizable portion of their winnings to him that night, that **his** boss might institute the mafia pension plan. He knew that he had the family trapped. But he forgot the undeniable fact that lawyers and teenage girls always have cell phones. It's the law.

"I know you're all in there. Johnny, why don't you bring your fat ass out here and we can renegotiate our contract?"

Cupping his hand around his mouth to direct his shout, Johnny B answered:

"Give me fifteen minutes. I've got to check on my family, Wilkes."

"Fair enough, but if you're not out here in fifteen, we're coming in…and you don't want that."

God bless that American invention: the phone tree. Sure, we all hate it when a distant acquaintance sends you one of those 'send this email to twenty people or Arabs will kidnap your gerbil' chain letters. But, in rare cases, the phone tree can be a good thing.

Trying desperately to keep from pissing his pants, Butler helped Mike and a surprisingly sober Uncle P push the rest of the heavy stuff to the door barricade.

The moon was half full that night. The crickets were silent. A stray cat walked leisurely up to the parking lot, surveyed the scene, and decided that he wasn't interested.

"Five more minutes in there, boys!!"

Back in the freezer section, Dee, Sparkles, Hannah and Oh-Oh were huddled together for warmth and desperate companionship. Hannah gazed at her daughter with love for the first time in as long as either could remember. Dee allowed herself a slight, momentary smile, but reality sets back in fast when there are bullets involved. Oh-Oh ate handfuls of delicious frost with his usual reckless abandon.

Two of Wilkes' bodyguards fired at the first F-150 that skidded to a 'Dukes of Hazard style 90 degree slide and stop' to arrive in the parking lot. They didn't expect the driver to fire back. Six more pickups, each complete with a gun rack and a driver with a burning desire to kill something, followed the first. Four armed men on foot simply emerged from the woods behind the store. When Nestor and his eldest son, Julio, set off the C-4 that Uncle P had stolen from the police station, thinking it was opium, a hole opened up in the back of the store large enough for the women and children to crawl through. Nestor led the women through the woods and to safety in broken Spanglish. They were out of harm's way, Nestor had cemented Hannah's love for all time, and now Elaine's had a service entrance.

As four more pickups full of armed and angry rednecks surrounded the parking lot, it dawned on Wilkes' henchmen that tonight might not go according to plan. Johnny B lifted his head above the wall, eye level with the bottom of the shattered window, and shouted to Wilkes:

"Drop it Wilkes and tell your boys to do the same!"

Not seeing any other option, Wilkes nodded at his men and dropped his gun. His boys followed suit. Then Johnny B, Dumpy, Mike and Butler walked calmly out into the parking lot with puffed chests and an air of after the storm calm. Uncle P would've joined them, but he was too busy sniffing a line of powdered rat poison he saw against the wall in the school supply aisle.

"Howdy, Wilkes. How's it going, partner?"

Wilkes glared at Johnny B and Dumpy with eyes alight with a deadly passion. They just smiled at him.

"You know, Wilkes. We've talked it over and I don't think we'll be needing your services after all."

"What are you going to do you, call the cops?"

"The cops? Where's the fun in that? Butler."

"Well Mr. Wilkes, it's doubtful that you four would spend much time in jail. I'm sure you've got top of the line defense attorneys. And I know that back room judicial deals still happen, not as often as they used to, but they do. So, instead…"

"He's all right for a lawyer, doncha think? A little wordy, but whatever. And Wilkes, a little advice for your coworkers, hoss. Don't mess with rednecks. We live for this shit."

They say that in the days of the firing squad, one of the gunmen would always have blanks, so that no one would ever know exactly who fired the killing shot. The same principle applies when sixteen gunmen fire round after round into the bodies of four 'recently retired' gangsters. They then buried the bodies in the woods behind the store.

Afterward, a secrecy pact was put into place. It didn't last, but, if there aren't any bodies, and the 'victims' are mobsters, and worse yet, Yankees, then the cops can be forgiven for shrugging and looking the other way.

And life went on in Comment, Georgia.

True or not, America has long billed itself as a classless society…

SOURCE MATERIAL

---<u>Merriam Webster's Collegiate Dictionary, Eleventh Edition,</u> Merriam-Webster Inc., Springfield, MA, 2003.

---Jacobs, A. J., <u>The Know-It-All: One Man's Humble Quest to Become the Smartest Person in the World.</u>, Simon & Schuster Paperbacks, New York, 2004.

(This is an awesome book)

---Music---thanks to Confederate Railroad, Tom Petty, my hero Jimmy Buffet, Patsy Cline, Twisted Sister, Dolly Parton, Hank Williams, Alabama, Paul Simon (you're so much better than Garfunkle), and The Fat Boys.

---life---looking around at my family, people with whom I grew up—basically I'm calling my eyes reference material, which is kind of conceited

---My wonderfully supportive family and their infinite patience with their black sheep

AUTHOR BIO

First time author, Bowen Craig, once broke into The Four Corners, the worst tourist trap since The Bermuda Rhombus and that Historical Marker immortalizing a Seven Secrets of Highly Successful People seminar run by KC and the Sunshine Band and the Unibomber (they teach you how to do a little dance, make a little love, get down tonight and blow shit up). The author acknowledges that breaking into a national monument doesn't exactly increase his street-cred. First off, it's in the middle of a Navajo reservation and those guys are pretty laid back. The author even got busted by a res cop, but he was just so damn cool. He waited until I'd finished taking pictures of my feet and then led me out—no show me your ID, no hollow threat of incarceration, just a leathery smile and a haggard 'come on, white boy, get out of here' spiel. All cops should be that guy.

Second, it's just a stupid, stupid tourist trap. 'Check it out, kids, it's a spot where four imaginary lines touch. Honey, come quick and take a picture. My feet are in Colorado and my hands are in Utah'. It's like Twister only without the possibility of sex.